ERIKA ZAMBELLO

BACKYARD SCIENCE & DISCOVERY WORKBOOK

SOUTH

ADVENTURE PUBLICATIONS

TABLE OF CONTENTS

ABOUT THIS BOOK

From the soaring Blue Ridge, Smoky, and Appalachian Mountain ranges and the sugar-sand beaches of the Florida and Alabama coastlines to the swamps, wetlands, and cypress forests of Louisiana and Texas, the South is home to many different ecosystems and supports thousands of fantastic and rare species. Covering 14 states, the region includes two distinct coastlines and ranges in elevation from more than 6,000 feet to beneath the waves, where you'll find the country's only hard coral reefs.

As a National Geographic Young Explorer and writer, I have traveled across the South visiting research sites, state and national parks, and wildlife refuges, always keeping a special eye on the biodiversity of each location.

Yet I experience the most joy when identifying species from my own home in North Florida. With a warm climate, distinct seasons, and plenty of rain, the South is an exceptional place to learn about backyard species. By turning your gaze to the yard behind your house or your local park, both you and your parents will be surprised at the intricate communities that share our landscapes with us.

This book features **19 hands-on science projects**, including raising native caterpillars, making mushroom spore prints, and attracting moths and other insects with an ultraviolet light; **more than 20 simple, fun introductions** to the region's habitats, birds, seasons, and rocks and minerals; and **11 fun activities** to help you make hypotheses, observe nature, and learn about the world around you.

Discover, explore, and share your remarkable observations as a family. You're going to be amazed at what you find!

Erika Zambello

GEOGRAPHY OF THE SOUTH

The South covers 14 states in all and stretches from the eastern parts of Texas and Oklahoma to the shores of the Atlantic Ocean and the Gulf of Mexico. Practice your geography and label the states above. Bonus points if you can name the state capitals of each one.

Answers on page 147!

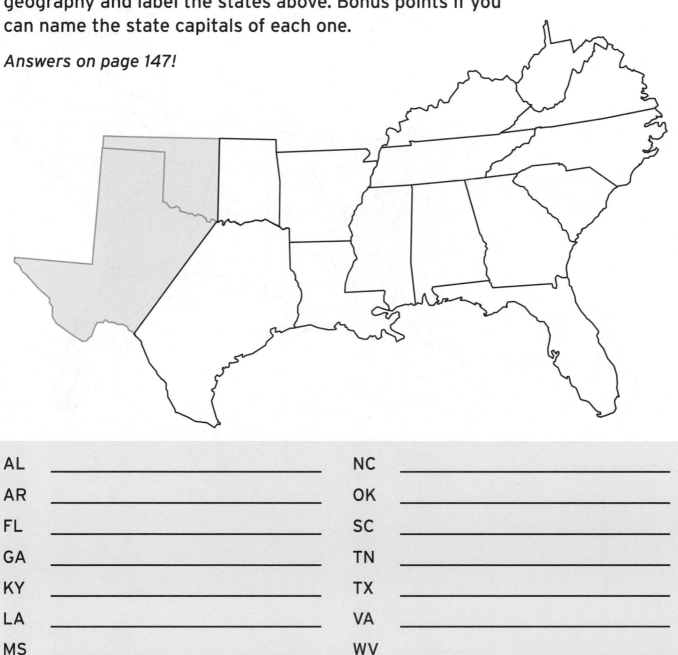

AL	_____	NC	_____
AR	_____	OK	_____
FL	_____	SC	_____
GA	_____	TN	_____
KY	_____	TX	_____
LA	_____	VA	_____
MS	_____	WV	_____

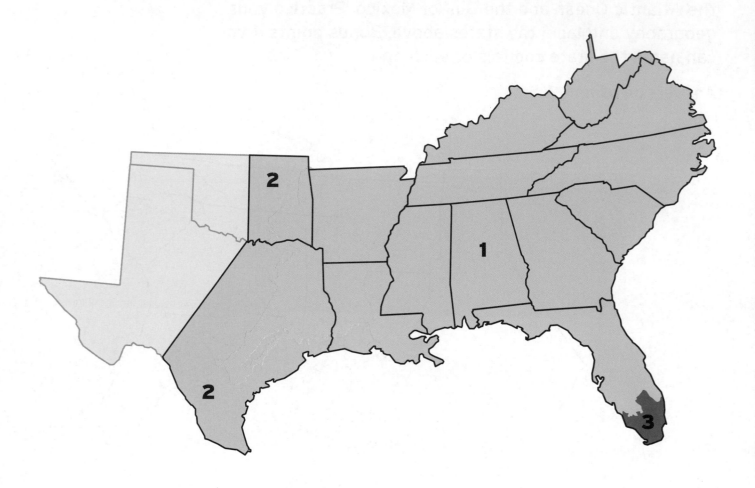

GET TO KNOW THE SOUTH'S BIOMES

The best way to get to know your Southern state and backyard is by understanding your natural neighborhood: its **biome**. A biome is a community of animals and plants that live in a specific kind of climate and environment.

You've probably heard of some biomes before: grasslands, forests, and so on.

The South is home to several different biomes:

1. Eastern Temperate Forest

2. Great Plains

3. Tropical Wet Forest

QUICK QUESTION

Which biome do you live in?

_____

_____

_____

GREAT PLAINS

Grasslands make up America's Great Plains. Stretching from the southern tip of Texas and well into Canada, the plains support some of the country's iconic species, including bison, elk, and more. European settlers initially viewed the prairies as "wastelands" and immediately set about converting the land, and its valuable soil, to farmland. Today, only a tiny fraction of these grasslands remains, and many of the animals and plants that depended on them have been **extirpated**, or are no longer present in this area.

In the South, the plains are limited to Texas and western Louisiana, flowing until they reach the Gulf of Mexico. These grasslands provide critical habitat for wintering **waterfowl**, which is another name for ducks, geese, and other birds that live on or near water.

QUICK QUIZ

Which of the following birds is a waterfowl species?

A. Fulvous Whistling-Duck

B. Northern Mockingbird

C. American Crow

D. Red-Tailed Hawk

Answer on page 147!

1. Grasslands are made up of different species of grasses. How many species of grasses can you find near your house?

_____

_____

_____

_____

2. Look up, do you see birds flying overhead? Write down the family groups of the birds you see: waterfowl, songbirds, wading birds, or raptors (birds like eagles, hawks, and owls).

_____

_____

_____

_____

TEMPERATE FORESTS

The word **temperate** means mild or moderate; in temperate forests, there are long periods (summer!) where the weather is warm. These forests primarily have deciduous trees (trees that lose their leaves), such as maples, hickories, and oaks, though **conifers** can grow there (sometimes in huge numbers) as well. Temperate forests are home to familiar creatures such as raccoons, woodpeckers, and White-Tailed Deer, but they also have thousands of species of insects, fungi, and plants.

Farmers once cut huge sections of Southern forests to make way for both livestock and crops. However, since then much of this biome has been allowed to grow back; that means these are **second-growth forests**.

QUICK QUIZ

There are many different kinds of trees in the South's deciduous forests, but tulip trees, oaks, and sweetgum are very common.

Can you identify each tree's leaves?

1. _____   2. _____   3. _____

Answers on page 147!

1. How many different deciduous trees (trees that lose their leaves) can you find near you?

_____

2. Which one is your favorite? Why?

_____

_____

TROPICAL WET FOREST

With average year-round temperatures well above freezing, the plant and animal communities within the tropical wet forest don't have to worry about frost. High temperatures, combined with plenty of rain, mean these forests are some of the most **biodiverse** on the planet. (That means the forests have many different kinds of plant and animal species.)

In the South, only the southern tip of Florida is part of this biome. On the coasts, mangrove forests—complete with three species of mangrove trees—protect the land from erosion while providing habitat for some of the most unique species in the United States. Roseate Spoonbills, for example, are bright-pink wading birds with a spatula-like bill, and they are common in this region.

As climate change causes stronger storms to impact South Florida, mangroves protect both the shoreline as well as coastal towns and cities.

QUICK QUIZ

What pink bird species lives in Florida's Tropical Wet Forest? (**Note:** Only one of the birds below lives in our region; the rest live in other countries.)

A. Scarlet Ibis

B. Pink Robin

C. Roseate Spoonbill

D. Rose-Breasted Cockatoo

Answer on page 147!

1. Tropical wet forests can grow near salt, fresh, or brackish water (which is a mix of fresh and salt water). What kind of water can you find near your backyard?

_____

_____

2. Tropical wet forests are known for the biodiversity of their plant life. Can you sketch a plant from your backyard?

THEN VS. NOW

The South was once largely covered with forests that stretched to the wetland meadows of the coastal plains. Indigenous peoples burned certain areas of the forests to create additional hunting territory, and lightning strikes naturally burned other sections of forests every few years. In fact, many of the pine woodlands of Florida, Georgia, and Alabama need to be periodically burned in order to maintain healthy ecosystems. This burning creates what is known as a **prescribed fire**.

However, European-descended settlers cut much of these forests for farms, **turpentine** (an oily liquid with many uses) and development, and forest managers of the nineteenth and twentieth centuries largely stopped the fires these forests need. Only in the late twentieth and the current twenty-first centuries have foresters, landowners, and scientists teamed up to restore Longleaf Pine ecosystems. These open pinelands provide habitat for rare species, including Red-Cockaded Woodpeckers and Flatwoods Salamanders.

Farther north, the American Chestnut tree once grew across 200 million acres of eastern forests, from the South all the way up to Maine. American Chestnuts can grow to nearly 100 feet tall, and its nuts acted as critical food sources for approximately 60 species of wildlife. Unfortunately, in the early 1900s an imported bark fungus took hold among the trees, and within 50 years had killed nearly every American Chestnut in the United States.

Imported insects and other pathogens continue to decimate our **native** trees. In the more recent past, for example, the Woolly Adelgid Beetle has nearly wiped out Hemlock trees.

QUICK QUIZ

How many species depended on the American Chestnut tree for food?

A. 12

B. 30

C. 60

D. 100

E. 1000

Answer on page 147!

STATE SYMBOLS

Another good way to get to know the region is by learning your state's official symbols. From the state bird and flower, which you might know already, to lesser-known categories, such as state amphibian, gemstone, or fossil, these iconic plants, animals, and materials have a long history with their states. Of course, not every state has symbols for the same categories—some states even have a state soil!—and some have many while others recognize only a handful. How many can you identify?

Why are state symbols important? Because they tell a story! By voting on symbols, elected officials and citizens are highlighting what makes their states—and their homes—special.

ALABAMA

Northern Flicker (Yellowhammer)

Bird

Oak-Leaf Hydrangea

Wildflower

Camellia

Flower

Marble

Rock

Tarpon

Saltwater Fish

Largemouth Bass

Freshwater Fish

Monarch Butterfly

Insect

Southern Longleaf Pine

Tree

Black Bear

Mammal

STATE SYMBOLS

MISSISSIPPI

Mockingbird
Bird

Petrified Wood
Stone

Southern Magnolia
Tree and Flower

Spicebush Swallowtail
Butterfly

Largemouth Bass
Fish

White-Tailed Deer
Land Mammal

Honeybee
Insect

American Alligator
Reptile

LOUISIANA

Brown Pelican

Bird

Magnolia

Flower

Alligator

Reptile

Bald Cypress

Tree

Louisiana Black Bear

Mammal

Honeybee

Insect

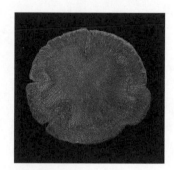

Petrified Palmwood

Fossil

Cabochon-Cut Oyster Shell (LaPearlite)

Gemstone

Agate

Mineral

STATE SYMBOLS

TEXAS

Mockingbird

Bird

Bluebonnet

Flower

Petrified Palmwood

Stone

Pecan

Tree

Monarch Butterfly

Insect

Texas Horned Lizard

Reptile

ARKANSAS

Mockingbird

Bird

Diamond

Gem/Stone

Quartz

Mineral

Loblolly Pine

Tree

Diana Fritillary

Butterfly

Honeybee

Insect

Apple Blossom

Flower

STATE SYMBOLS

OKLAHOMA

Scissor-Tailed Flycatcher

Bird

Collared Lizard

Reptile

Oklahoma Rose

Flower

Black Swallowtail

Butterfly

Honeybee

Insect

Indian Blanket

Wildflower

Eastern Redbud

Tree

Barite Rose

Rock

FLORIDA

Northern Mockingbird

Bird

Orange Blossom

Flower

Sabal Palm

Tree

Agatized Coral

Stone

Manatee

Marine Mammal

Florida Panther

Animal

American Alligator

Reptile

Zebra Longwing

Butterfly

STATE SYMBOLS

SOUTH CAROLINA

Carolina Wren

Bird

Yellow Jessamine

Flower

Cabbage Palmetto

Tree

Blue Granite

Stone

Tiger Swallowtail

Butterfly

Carolina Mantis

Insect

White-Tailed Deer

Mammal

GEORGIA

Brown Thrasher

Bird

Gopher Tortoise

Reptile

Tiger Swallowtail

Butterfly

Cherokee Rose

Flower

Largemouth Bass

Freshwater Fish

Honeybee

Insect

Staurolite

Mineral

Live Oak

Tree

Azalea

Wildflower

STATE SYMBOLS

NORTH CAROLINA

Cardinal

Bird

Dogwood

Flower

Honeybee

Insect

Gray Squirrel

Mammal

Granite

Rock

Pine

Tree

Eastern Tiger Swallowtail

Butterfly

Carolina Lily

Wildflower

Eastern Box Turtle

Reptile

VIRGINIA

Northern Cardinal
Bird

American Dogwood
Flower

Tiger Swallowtail
Butterfly

American Dogwood
Tree

Brook Trout
Freshwater Fish

Striped Bass
Saltwater Fish

Nelsonite
Rock

STATE SYMBOLS

WEST VIRGINIA

Cardinal
Bird

Sugar Maple
Tree

Black Bear
Animal

Rhododendron
Flower

Honeybee
Insect

Monarch
Butterfly

Lithostrotionella
Fossil

TENNESSEE

Mockingbird

Bird

Zebra Swallowtail

Butterfly

Iris

State Cultivated Flower

Passionflower

Wildflower

Tennessee Coneflower

Wildflower

Tennessee Pearl

Gem

Firefly

Insect*

Eastern Box Turtle

Reptile

Limestone

Rock

Tulip Poplar

Tree

Raccoon

Wild Animal

*Tennessee actually has three state insects: the firefly; the ladybug; and the honeybee, the state agricultural insect.

STATE SYMBOLS

KENTUCKY

Cardinal

Bird

Brachiopod

Fossil

Butterfly

Butterfly

Goldenrod

Flower

Coal

Mineral

Tulip Poplar

Tree

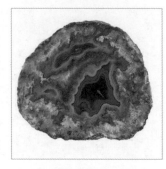

Kentucky Agate

Rock

QUICK QUIZ

Many Southern states share their state birds. Which state below has not chosen the cardinal as its state bird?

A. Kentucky

B. Virginia

C. Georgia

D. West Virginia

Answer on page 147!

1. Many states identify official state trees. Do you have one (or more) state trees in your yard? If you do, list them below!

_____

_____

_____

2. Many states choose birds that are easy to find and identify as their state symbol. Have you ever seen your state (or another state's bird) in your neighborhood? If you have, list them below.

_____

_____

_____

_____

INTRODUCED VS. INVASIVE

Because of its warmer temperatures, the South hosts many plants and animals that were **introduced** to the region. Some of these, such as agricultural crops or livestock, were introduced on purpose; they are **nonnative,** but they haven't been a problem. Others were introduced on purpose or by accident, but once they arrived they spread quickly, often finding an environment with few predators or natural checks on their population. These species then became **invasive,** spreading uncontrollably and either eating native animals and plants or taking over their food sources and habitat.

Invasive species are a special problem for Florida, where temperatures often do not dip below freezing, even in the winter.

How can you prevent the spread of invasive species? Never release pets of any kind outside if you can no longer take care of them. Also, please choose native plants for your garden. (Plants can "escape" from gardens too!)

Pictured here are a few familiar but invasive plants and animals.

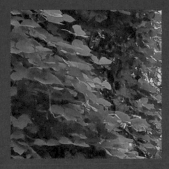

Kudzu

Lionfish

Pythons

Japanese
Climbing Fern

House Sparrow

Feral Hog

Iguanas

QUICK QUIZ

Which of the following animals is an introduced species in the South?

A. Texas Horned Lizard

B. American Alligator

C. Iguana

D. Green Anole

Answer on page 147!

Can you think of other introduced species in your area?
Hint: Most farm animals aren't from here! The same is true for many weeds.

_____

_____

_____

_____

_____

_____

_____

_____

_____

GETTING TO KNOW
YOUR WEATHER

You probably know what a hot summer day is like, but what's the hottest you remember? Ninety degrees, maybe 100? What do you think the highest temperature recorded anywhere in your state was? (**Note:** It probably didn't reach this temperature in the place you live, but it did happen *somewhere* in your state.)

MAKE A HYPOTHESIS*

1. What was the highest maximum temperature in my state?

   My guess:_____

2. OK, and you've felt cold, too, maybe shivering at the bus stop or walking to school. So what do you think the coldest temperature recorded anywhere in your state is?

   Coldest temperature in my state?

   My guess: _____

3. And do you like running out in the rain? Me too. But how much rain do you think fell on your state's rainiest day? A foot? Even more? (Don't forget that hurricane rains count!)

   What was the maximum rainfall in my state during one day?

   My guess: _____

*A **hypothesis** is a guess you make based on information you already know.

A FEW SOUTHERN WEATHER RECORDS

STATE			DATE
Alabama	Maximum Temperature	112°F	Sep 6, 1925
Alabama	Minimum Temperature	-27°F	Jan 30, 1966
Alabama	24-Hour Precipitation	32.52"	July 19-20, 1997
Arkansas	Maximum Temperature	120°F	Aug 10, 1936
Arkansas	Minimum Temperature	-29°F	Feb 13, 1905
Arkansas	24-Hour Precipitation	14.06"	Dec 3, 1982
Florida	Maximum Temperature	109°F	June 29, 1931
Florida	Minimum Temperature	-2°F	Feb 13, 1899
Florida	24-Hour Precipitation	23.28"	Nov 11-12, 1980
Georgia	Maximum Temperature	112°F	July 24, 1952 Aug 20, 1983
Georgia	Minimum Temperature	-17°F	Jan 27, 1940
Georgia	24-Hour Precipitation	21.1"	July 6, 1994
Kentucky	Maximum Temperature	114°F	July 28, 1930
Kentucky	Minimum Temperature	-37°F	Jan 19, 1994

Data: ncdc.noaa.gov/extremes/scec/records

A FEW SOUTHERN WEATHER RECORDS

STATE NAME	ELEMENT	VALUE	DATE
Kentucky	24-Hour Precipitation	10.48"	March 1, 1997
Louisiana	Maximum Temperature	114°F	Aug 10, 1936
Louisiana	Minimum Temperature	-16°F	Feb 13, 1899
Louisiana	24-Hour Precipitation	22"	Aug 28-29, 1962
Mississippi	Maximum Temperature	115°F	July 29, 1930
Mississippi	Minimum Temperature	-19°F	Jan 30, 1966
Mississippi	24-Hour Precipitation	15.68"	July 9, 1968
North Carolina	Maximum Temperature	110°F	Aug 21, 1983
North Carolina	Minimum Temperature	-34°F	Jan 21, 1985
North Carolina	24-Hour Precipitation	22.22"	July 15-16, 1916
Oklahoma	Maximum Temperature	120°F	Aug 10, 1936 Aug 12, 1936 July 18, 1936 July 18, 1936
Oklahoma	Minimum Temperature	-31°F	Feb 10, 2011
Oklahoma	24-Hour Precipitation	15.68"	Oct 11, 1973

STATE NAME	ELEMENT	VALUE	DATE
South Carolina	Maximum Temperature	113°F	June 29, 2012
South Carolina	Minimum Temperature	-19°F	Jan 21, 1985
South Carolina	24-Hour Precipitation	14.8"	Sept 16, 1999
Tennessee	Maximum Temperature	113°F	Aug 9, 1930 July 29, 1930
Tennessee	Minimum Temperature	-32°F	Dec 30, 1917
Tennessee	24-Hour Precipitation	13.6"	Sept 13, 1982
Texas	Maximum Temperature	120°F	Aug 12, 1936 June 28, 1994
Texas	Minimum Temperature	-23°F	Feb 12, 1899 Feb 8, 1933
Texas	24-Hour Precipitation	42"	July 25-26, 1979
Virginia	Maximum Temperature	110°F	July 5, 1900 July 7, 1900 July 15, 1954
Virginia	Minimum Temperature	-30°F	Jan 21, 1985
Virginia	24-Hour Precipitation	14.28"	Sept 16, 1999
West Virginia	Maximum Temperature	112°F	Aug 4, 1930 July 10, 1936
West Virginia	Minimum Temperature	-37°F	Dec 30, 1917
West Virginia	24-Hour Precipitation	12.02"	June 18, 1949

IS THE SUN SETTING EARLIER?!

In winter, you've probably noticed how it gets darker earlier. That happens because the Earth is tilted on its axis, so certain parts of the planet get more daylight in some seasons, than in others. If you've traveled to the north or to the south of where you live, you've probably noticed that the amount of daylight varies with **latitude** (how far north or south you are from the equator).

MAKE A HYPOTHESIS

1. What month do you think has the shortest day of the year in the South?

_____

2. Which month has the longest day of the year in the South?

_____

3. On the shortest day of the year where you live, what time is sunset?

_____

LONGEST & SHORTEST DAYS
ACROSS THE SOUTH

The longest day of the year in the South is known as the **summer solstice;** that's when the North Pole has its maximum tilt toward the sun. The shortest day in the South is known as the **winter solstice;** that's when the North Pole is tilted away the most from the sun.

The date that each solstice occurs varies a little each year, but the summer solstice in the northern hemisphere always occurs between June 20 and June 22, and the winter solstice is always between December 20 and December 23.

Here and on the next page, the text to the right shows when the sun will rise and set in several places across the South during an upcoming winter and summer solstice. The first location is in the far northern part of the South, the second is roughly in the middle of the region, and the third locale is in the far southern portion of the region.

WINTER SOLSTICE

Northern West Virginia (39.6295° N, 79.9559° W)
December 21
Sunrise: 7:37 am
Sunset: 4:59 pm

Central Georgia (33.7490° N, 84.3880° W)
December 21
Sunrise: 7:39 am
Sunset: 5:33 pm

Southern Florida (24.5551° N, 81.7800° W)
December 21
Sunrise: 7:07 am
Sunset: 5:44 pm

Data: esrl.noaa.gov/gmd/grad/solcalc/

LONGEST & SHORTEST DAYS ACROSS THE SOUTH

In southern Florida during the winter solstice, the sun rises a full half hour earlier than in northern West Virginia, and the sun stays out nearly 45 minutes later!

Why are the changing sunset and sunrise times important? It's true that sunrise and sunset help you know when to wake up and go to sleep, but for animals and wildlife, these times are even more important! Birds and other critters use sunrise and sunset to tell them what time of year it is and whether they should be breeding, feeding their young, or migrating.

SUMMER SOLSTICE

Northern West Virginia (39.6295° N, 79.9559° W)
June 20
Sunrise: 5:52 am
Sunset: 8:51 pm

Central Georgia (33.7490° N, 84.3880° W)
June 20
Sunrise: 6:27 am
Sunset: 8:51 pm

Southern Florida (24.5551° N, 81.7800° W)
June 20
Sunrise: 6:39 am
Sunset: 8:19 pm

Sunrise lights up the mountains.

The sun rises in Atlanta, Georgia.

HURRICANES

The South, especially the states bordering the Atlantic Ocean and the Gulf of Mexico, faces hurricanes almost every year. Hurricane season runs from June 1 through November 30.

When warm water rises over the tropics, cooler air is displaced. As the cooler air is then warmed, the cycle can create large storm clouds, eventually forming hurricanes.

Hurricanes can cause damage not only to the coast but also to inland forests and ecosystems. However, some species depend on hurricanes to thrive. Along Florida's coast, hurricanes reduce vegetation on dunes that border the beach, creating better nesting habitat for seabirds and shorebirds.

Unfortunately, as climate change continues to make our oceans warmer, hurricanes are predicted to become more frequent and more intense.

GET TO KNOW THE SEASONS & THE WEATHER

The seasons of the year are like the hours on a clock: winter is the night, spring is the morning, summer is the afternoon, and fall is twilight. If you pay attention to this seasonal clock, and the animals and plants found during each season, you'll be studying **phenology**. Phenology is the study of the cycles of the seasons and the natural world over time. By studying the phenology of your area—for example, when certain birds arrive in spring, when raspberries are first ripe in summer, or when it starts to really get cold—you'll learn a lot about the natural world around you and what to expect next.

START OUT BY MAKING SOME PREDICTIONS

Before you start observing, see what you already know. Make some predictions about when you expect to see the wildlife around you. You might not have seen all of these animals or plants before. If not, that's OK, but make predictions about those you recognize.

Robins don't always migrate away during the winter, but they definitely are easier to spot during some months of the year.

1. What season do you notice robins in the most?

_____

_____

2. In which month?

_____

_____

American Robin

3. In which month do dogwoods bloom where you live?

_____

_____

4. In which month(s) do the trees get their leaves where you live?

_____

_____

5. When do they lose them?

_____

6. When do raspberries get ripe where you live?

_____

7. When do blueberries get ripe where you live?

_____

8. In which month(s) do you see Monarch Butterflies?

_____

_____

9. When does it normally snow where you live? Does it snow at all?

_____

10. Which months does it never or rarely snow in?

_____

Dogwoods

Raspberries

Blueberries

Monarch Butterfly

DO-IT-YOURSELF PHENOLOGY

The easiest way to start out with phenology is by observing one type of plant or animal throughout the year. Try this with the plants or animals in your yard. For example, if you have a maple tree or an oak nearby, keep track of when it loses it leaves, and then, in the spring, when the buds emerge, flowers and leaves form, and when fruit (seeds or acorns) develops. Then keep track of when the tree loses its leaves. Jot down a few notes about the weather over the past few days, too, as rain and temperature often have a major effect on these regular changes in nature.

It's easy to do: find a tree in your yard, and then write down the dates that you notice the following changes.

Year:_____

Buds form: _____

Flowers form: _____

Leaves emerge: _____

Seeds form:_____

Tree is fully "leafed out":_____

Leaves change colors in fall:_____

Leaves start falling off tree:_____

Then keep track of that same tree the next year, and see how different those same dates are. Does the tree have buds the same day of each year? How about seeds? What was the weather like?

Year:_____

Buds form: _____

Flowers form: _____

Leaves emerge: _____

Seeds form:_____

Tree is fully "leafed out":_____

Leaves change colors in fall:_____

Leaves start falling off tree: _____

PHENOLOGY CALENDAR: SPRING

These are the average dates that these natural events occur; they can vary each year, and by location, so keep track of when you spot these plants, animals, and events near you!

MARCH

- Oaks, maples, and beech trees are showing buds and leaves
- Wax Myrtles begin to flower
- Many bird species have already begun to nest
- Bald Cypresses develop open pollen cones
- Cotton planting begins
- Firefly season begins
- Red Maples bloom

What I spotted in March:

_____

_____

_____

_____

_____

_____

_____

Northern Cardinal nest

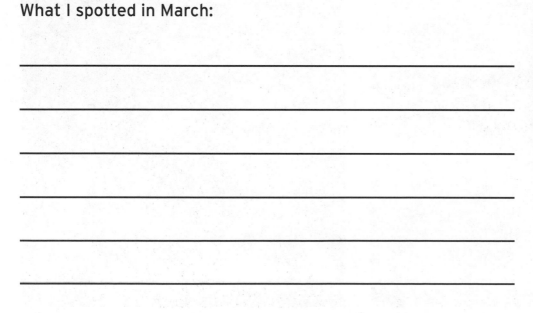

Wax Myrtle flowers

APRIL

- Leaves of deciduous trees continue to grow
- Dogwoods have open flowers
- Eastern Redbuds bloom
- Mayflies are active and mating
- Tulip Trees show colored leaves and open flowers
- Large groups of migratory birds move north through the South
- Loblolly Pines enter their peak pollen period

What I spotted in April:

_____

_____

_____

_____

_____

_____

_____

_____

_____

Hooded Warbler

Loblolly Pine pollen

Redbud flowers

Dogwood flowers

All phenology data: www.usanpn.org/data

MAY

- Wild blueberries begin to ripen
- Sea Turtles begin nesting
- Hummingbirds are active
- Bald Eagle nesting season ends
- Tree frogs are in breeding season

What I spotted in May:

_____

_____

_____

_____

_____

_____

Blueberries

Sea Turtle nest

Bald Eagle chicks

Ruby-Throated Hummingbird

PHENOLOGY CALENDAR: SUMMER

JUNE

- Chanterelle mushrooms begin to appear
- Wild berries, including strawberries and blackberries, ripen
- Firefly season ends
- Hurricane season begins
- Black Cherry fruits ripen and drop
- Northern Cardinals are busy with multiple broods

What I spotted in June:

_____

_____

_____

_____

_____

_____

_____

Chanterelle mushrooms

Blackberries

Hurricane

JULY

- Cotton harvesting begins
- Cardinal Flower begins blooming with bright red petals
- July marks the middle of seabird- and shorebird-nesting season: birds are on the beach, and parents may nest once more

AUGUST

- American Beautyberry forms bright-purple berries
- End of bird nesting season
- Cool temperatures can signal the start of Monarch migration

What I spotted in July and August:

_____

_____

_____

_____

_____

_____

_____

Cotton

Monarch

American Beautyberry

Black Skimmer

Cardinal Flower

Empty nest

PHENOLOGY CALENDAR: FALL

SEPTEMBER

- Sugarcane harvest begins
- Leaves begin turning colors, especially in higher elevations
- Hickory nuts ripen and fall

Changing tree leaves

Sugarcane

What I spotted in September:

_____

_____

_____

_____

_____

_____

Shagbark Hickory nuts

Red Maple

OCTOBER

- Migratory birds pass through the South on their way to their wintering grounds
- Bald Eagle nesting season begins
- Wintering waterfowl arrive
- Bald Cypress needles begin turning from green to gold
- Eastern Redbuds bear fruit

NOVEMBER

- Hurricane season ends
- Most migrating birds have long since left
- Manatees begin to migrate to freshwater springs in search of warmer water temperatures

What I spotted in October and November:

_____

_____

_____

_____

_____

_____

_____

_____

_____

Summer Tanager

Bald Cypress

Manatee

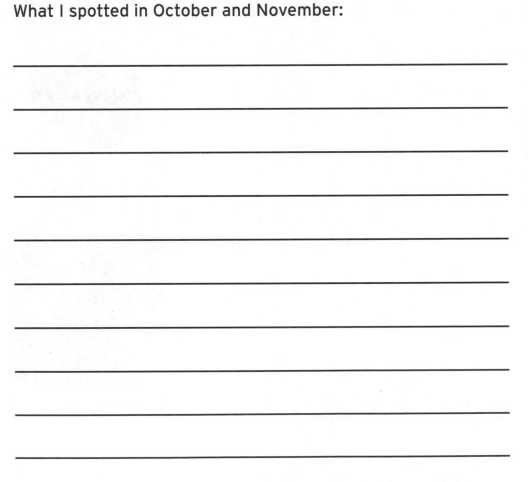

PHENOLOGY CALENDAR: WINTER

DECEMBER

- Bobcat breeding season begins
- Switchgrass can offer pasture and grazing for livestock
- North Atlantic Right Whales begin delivering calves off the Georgia and Florida Atlantic coastline

Bobcat

JANUARY

- Cold temperatures can cause frost as far south as Florida
- Purple Martins return from their wintering grounds
- The earliest Swallow-Tailed Kites appear
- Great Horned Owls begin laying eggs
- Wood Frogs begin breeding

Purple Martin

FEBRUARY

- Breeding season for Burrowing Owls begins
- Great Blue Herons nesting season begins

What I spotted in the winter:

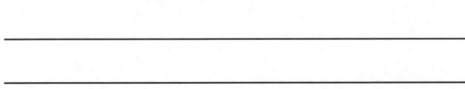

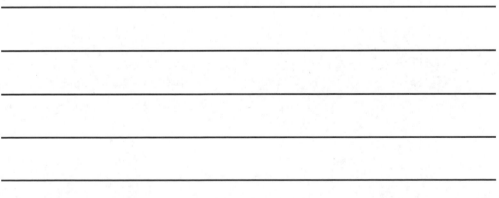

Burrowing Owl

YOUR STATE'S MAJOR FARM CROPS & FARM PRODUCTS

After settlement, much of the South became farmland. Along with animals raised for food and dairy products, a wide variety of crops are grown in the South, from tomatoes and sugarcane in Florida to hay and soybeans in Kentucky and Tennessee. Below are the top crops, or **commodities (agricultural products),** in the South.

ALABAMA

- Catfish
- Cattle
- Chickens
- Corn
- Cotton
- Eggs
- Peanuts
- Soybeans

MISSISSIPPI

- Catfish
- Cattle
- Chickens
- Cotton
- Eggs
- Soybeans

LOUISIANA

- Cattle
- Chickens
- Corn
- Rice
- Soybeans
- Sugarcane

TEXAS

- Cattle
- Chickens
- Corn
- Cotton
- Dairy/Milk
- Hay

ARKANSAS

- Chickens
- Corn
- Cows
- Eggs
- Rice
- Soybeans

OKLAHOMA

- Cattle
- Chickens
- Corn
- Cotton
- Hay
- Hogs
- Wheat

FLORIDA

- Cattle
- Dairy/Milk
- Flowers
- Oranges
- Sugarcane
- Tomatoes

GEORGIA

- Cattle
- Chickens
- Cotton
- Dairy/Milk
- Eggs
- Peanuts

SOUTH CAROLINA

- Cattle
- Chickens
- Corn
- Cotton
- Eggs
- Peaches

NORTH CAROLINA

- Chickens
- Eggs
- Hogs
- Tobacco
- Turkeys
- Soybeans

VIRGINIA

- Cattle
- Chickens
- Corn
- Dairy/Milk
- Soybeans
- Turkey

WEST VIRGINIA

- Cattle
- Chickens
- Corn
- Eggs
- Hay
- Turkey

TENNESSEE

- Cattle
- Chickens
- Corn
- Cotton
- Hay
- Soybeans

KENTUCKY

- Cattle
- Chickens
- Corn
- Hay
- Soybeans
- Tobacco

QUICK QUIZ

If you haven't lived near a farm or worked on one, you might not recognize the crops growing in the field. Can you identify each type of crop?

1. _____ 2. _____ 3. _____ 4. _____

Answers on page 147!

WHAT'S THE HIGHEST & LOWEST POINT IN YOUR STATE?

The South extends from the flat expanses of Florida to the tallest peaks in the Blue Ridge, Smoky, and Appalachian Mountains. When measuring a state's elevation, or that of a mountain or a hill, geographers compare a given place's elevation to that of sea level. So, for example, Florida's highest point—in the entire state—is just 345 feet above sea level. That's not exactly surprising, as it's surrounded by ocean.

What do you think the highest point is in your state? What about the lowest?

Highest: _____ feet above sea level

Lowest: _____ feet above sea level

FAST FACT

Visiting the highest point in an area is something of a growing hobby. Known as "highpointing," it's a fun way to get to know your state, and its quirks, a little better. Though in some places, such as Alaska, where the highest point is 20,310 feet, you'll definitely need a lot of experience, gear, and training before you ever make an attempt.

Data: www.usgs.gov/science-support/osqi/yes/resources-teachers/highest-and-lowest-elevations

ALABAMA

Highest Point
Above Sea Level:

2,407 feet

Mount Cheaha

Lowest Point
Above Sea Level:

0 feet

*Where Alabama
meets the Gulf
of Mexico*

MISSISSIPPI

Highest Point
Above Sea Level:

806 feet

Woodall Mountain

Lowest Point
Above Sea Level:

0 feet

*Where Mississippi
meets the Gulf
of Mexico*

LOUISIANA

Highest Point
Above Sea Level:

535 feet

Driskill Mountain

Lowest Point
Above Sea Level:

0 feet

*Where Louisiana
meets the Gulf
of Mexico*

TEXAS

Highest Point
Above Sea Level:

8,749 feet

Guadalupe Peak

Lowest Point
Above Sea Level:

0 feet

*Where Texas meets
the Gulf of Mexico*

Highest locations shown for each state.

HIGHEST & LOWEST POINTS

ARKANSAS

Highest Point
Above Sea Level:

2,753 feet
Mount Magazine

Lowest Point
Above Sea Level:

55 feet
Ouachita River

OKLAHOMA

Highest Point
Above Sea Level:

4,973 feet
Black Mesa

Lowest Point
Above Sea Level:

289 feet
Little River

FLORIDA

Highest Point
Above Sea Level:

345 feet
Britton Hill

Lowest Point
Above Sea Level:

0 feet
*Where Florida meets
the Gulf of Mexico and
Atlantic Ocean*

GEORGIA

Highest Point
Above Sea Level:

4,784 feet
Brasstown Bald

Lowest Point
Above Sea Level:

0 feet
*Where Georgia meets
the Atlantic Ocean*

*Highest locations shown for each state

SOUTH CAROLINA

Highest Point Above Sea Level:	Lowest Point Above Sea Level:
3,553 feet	**0 feet**
Sassafras Mountain Tower	*Where South Carolina meets the Atlantic Ocean*

NORTH CAROLINA

Highest Point Above Sea Level:	Lowest Point Above Sea Level:
6,684 feet	**0 feet**
Mount Mitchell	*Where North Carolina meets the Atlantic Ocean*

VIRGINIA

Highest Point Above Sea Level:	Lowest Point Above Sea Level:
5,729 feet	**0 feet**
Mount Rogers	*Where Virginia meets the Atlantic Ocean*

WEST VIRGINIA

Highest Point Above Sea Level:	Lowest Point Above Sea Level:
4,863 feet	**247 feet**
Spruce Knob	*Harpers Ferry*

*highest locations shown for each state

HIGHEST & LOWEST POINTS

KENTUCKY

Highest Point Above Sea Level:	Lowest Point Above Sea Level:
4,145 feet	**257 feet**
Black Mountain	*Mississippi River*

TENNESSEE

Highest Point Above Sea Level:	Lowest Point Above Sea Level:
6,643 feet	**178 feet**
Clingmans Dome	*Mississippi River*

Highest locations shown for each state.

DID YOU KNOW?

Different plants and animals prefer different elevations! Higher elevations tend to be colder, and they remain colder for a longer part of the year. Species have **adapted** to these conditions, and thrive here.

Because higher elevations resemble habitats in more-northern states, these mountainous areas are hot spots for birds you cannot find elsewhere in the South.

For example, Winter Wrens usually breed in the Northeast and into Canada, but they can be found year-round on Southern mountaintops! They look and act differently than Carolina Wrens, a related species that lives in lower elevations.

Winter Wren

Carolina Wren

SPOT YOUR STATE BIRD

BROWN PELICAN

State Bird of Louisiana

WHEN WILL I SEE THEM?
Once nearly extirpated from Louisiana, Brown Pelicans have made an impressive comeback. They can be seen year-round along Louisiana's coastline.

WILL THEY COME TO MY YARD?
Nope! They live and feed exclusively along the coast—but keep your eyes peeled for these large, brown birds during trips to the beach.

BROWN THRASHER

State Bird of Georgia

WHEN WILL I SEE THEM?
Brown Thrashers live in the South year-round, but they prefer to forage in dense thickets and undergrowth, making them more difficult to spot. They do, however, love to sing, so listen for a series of mimicking songs. They know thousands!

WILL THEY COME TO MY YARD?
Yes! They will visit feeders, especially if the seed falls to the ground. If feeders are close to dense vegetation, they are more likely to visit.

CAROLINA WREN

State Bird of South Carolina

WHEN WILL I SEE THEM?
Small but feisty, Carolina Wrens spend their lives in the South year-round. With brown wings and tail above and a buff-colored stomach, they are easily identified by their white eye stripe and upright tail.

WILL THEY COME TO MY YARD?
Add suet feeders to your yard during the winter months, and you will attract Carolina Wrens. Do you have a brush pile in your yard? Great! Wrens love to take shelter in the cracks and crevices of the overlapping branches.

NORTHERN CARDINAL

State Bird of North Carolina, Virginia, West Virginia, and Kentucky

WHEN WILL I SEE THEM?
One of America's brightest-colored species, Northern Cardinals spend the entire year throughout the eastern United States.

WILL THEY COME TO MY YARD?
Northern Cardinals love backyard bird feeders; they are particularly drawn to sunflower seeds. If you leave uncleared undergrowth in your backyard, including bushes and hedges, you may also attract nesting pairs! Males (pictured) are a brilliant red all over, while females are mostly tan with touches of red.

SPOT YOUR STATE BIRD

NORTHERN FLICKER (YELLOWHAMMER)

State Bird of Alabama

WHEN WILL I SEE THEM?
Northern Flickers are found year-round in Alabama and across the United States. In the summer months their range extends into Canada.

WILL THEY COME TO MY YARD?
Yes! Though they don't usually eat from feeders, they will use nest boxes and birdbaths, especially if your yard is near woodlands.

NORTHERN MOCKINGBIRD

State Bird of Mississippi, Florida, Texas, Arkansas, Tennessee

WHEN WILL I SEE THEM?
Northern Mockingbirds are incredibly common. They live year-round in the South, Northeast, and certain Southwestern states. They are loud, mimicking other birds as well as human noises like horns and car engines.

WILL THEY COME TO MY YARD?
Yes! They may not visit your feeder, but they have adapted well to suburban environments and can often be spotted singing from trees, lampposts, and rooftops. Plant mulberry or other fruiting bushes to attract them.

SCISSOR-TAILED FLYCATCHER

State Bird of Oklahoma

WHEN WILL I SEE THEM?

With an impressive tail, this flycatcher is a favorite among birders. During the summer months, Scissor-Tailed Flycatchers breed in Texas, Oklahoma, Kansas, Louisiana, Arkansas, and a smattering of other states.

WILL THEY COME TO MY YARD?

While Scissor-Tailed Flycatchers usually eat insects, they do occasionally stop at mulberry, hackberry, and other fruiting bushes. Plant these in your yard and watch for flycatchers!

1. Have you spotted your state bird? Where?

_____

_____

_____

2. What's your favorite state bird in the South?

_____

_____

_____

3. How about your favorite bird in your state?

_____

_____

_____

MAKE YOUR YARD BIRD-FRIENDLY

Lawns are pretty, but they don't do a lot to help birds, bugs, and most other kinds of wildlife. To really draw birds (and the insects they often eat!) to your yard, you and your parents can make your yard a bit wilder. It's pretty easy to start doing this. Here are a few tips:

PLANT NATIVE PLANTS

Whether you're planting native trees that provide cover, nesting sites, or fruit, or sunflowers that become snacking stations once they droop forward in late summer and fall, native plants are beacons to birds. For a list of what to plant, visit www.audubon.org/native-plants. To make sure you're finding the best native plants, look for a native-plant nursery near where you live.

PUT OUT A WATER SOURCE

Birds don't just need food—they need water too! A birdbath, especially one with a "water wiggler" (available at many birding or home improvement stores), is a great option. The movement of the water prevents mosquitoes from laying eggs in the water, and the sound of the moving water draws in birds from all over.

DON'T SPRAY YOUR YARD WITH BUG OR WEED KILLERS

Mosquitoes are really annoying, but the popular foggers or sprays that many people apply to their yards don't just kill mosquitoes. These insecticides often kill any bugs they touch, including bees, butterflies, and the many beetles and other creepy-crawlies that birds depend on for food. Pesticides and herbicides (weed killers) can also directly hurt birds.

American Beautyberry

Coneflower

Cardinal Flower

Birdbath

LEAVE OUT NEST-MAKING MATERIALS IN SPRING

Bird nests are pretty incredible, and it's even more impressive that birds make them using only their feet and their beaks!

WHAT TO DO

You can help them out by leaving natural, pesticide-free nesting materials in handy locations around your yard. Examples include soft, fluffy plant parts, such as the down from cattails, moss, or feathers you find on the ground (but make sure to wear gloves when picking those up). You can put these in easy-to-access places around your yard; on the ground, wedged into tree bark—or even hanging in an empty suet feeder.

Important Note: There are some things you don't want to give birds, especially human-made or synthetic products such as plastic, metal, or dryer lint. This includes most strings and yarns. And even though it came from our heads, no human hair or pet hair, please! Birds can get their feet and other body parts trapped in strings and hair, and dryer lint makes their nests too soggy when it rains. Human-made materials can also be **toxic** (poisonous) to birds, either if the bird eats some of these materials or if it absorbs some of the chemicals in the materials.

MAKE A RECIPE TO FEED TO BIRDS

If you get creative, you can feed birds a lot more than birdseed! Making your own bird food is a fun way to attract the birds you want to see.

Here are two options, although there are lots of others.

DO-IT-YOURSELF BIRDSEED MIX

A lot of the birdseed mixes sold in stores just aren't very good. Often, they contain lots of filler seeds (such as milo, a small, brown, round seed). Filler seeds don't have a lot of the nutrients that birds need, unlike seeds such as black-oil sunflower seeds, which are full of good stuff like protein, vitamins, and fats.

So what do you do? Make your own birdseed mix! Buy some black-oil sunflower seeds to use as your base, then add other seeds to those.

Here's a mix that works great for platform feeders. All of the ingredients are usually available at garden centers or home improvement stores.

WHAT YOU'LL NEED

- 4 cups black-oil sunflower seeds
- 1 cup peanut chips
- 1 cup cracked corn

WHAT TO DO

Mix it all together and place it on a hanging bird feeder. For an extra-tasty treat, you can also add in some sliced apples or plums.

A SIMPLE PEANUT BUTTER BIRDSEED FEEDER

WHAT YOU'LL NEED

• Pine cones

• Peanut butter

• Black-oil sunflower seeds or birdseed mix

• Some string

WHAT TO DO

This tried-and-true recipe really works. First, you'll need to collect some pine cones. Then mix some peanut butter, sunflower seeds, and dried mealworms in a bowl. Next, take the pine cones and push them into the peanut butter and seeds, making sure everything is mixed together well like in the picture. Now tie some string to the top of each pine cone, and hang it from a tree. You can do this as many times as you like.

If you can't find any pine cones, just mix the ingredients together, then "paint" or smear the mixture onto a tree's bark.

Make both kinds of feeders, then keep track of the birds that come to each one! Did different birds come to the different feeders?

_____

_____

_____

_____

DO A BACKYARD BIRD COUNT

If you're new to birding, chances are you probably haven't conducted a backyard bird count before. It's a simple activity, but it can teach you quite a bit about birds, including how to recognize their calls and when and where to look. It's also a lot of fun, and you might be surprised at what you find. Best of all, you don't need any gear at all, though a field guide, binoculars, and a smartphone camera can be handy.

WHAT YOU'LL NEED

- A notepad and pen/pencil to record your finds

- A field guide, binoculars, and a smartphone camera (optional)

WHAT TO DO

To conduct your count, give each participant a notebook, and pick a 15-minute time slot to look for birds. Go to your backyard (or even a balcony), and quietly look and listen for birds. Look near feeders, if you have them; see if you can spy birds flitting about in cover or perched in trees, and especially near garden areas (even potted plants or container gardens).

Wherever you are, but especially in the city or the suburbs, look for birds soaring overhead. A place where lots of people live might not seem like a birding hot spot, but because major cities are usually near rivers and have plenty of pigeons and songbirds, they're often home to nesting groups of birds like Peregrine Falcons, which hunt the other birds for food.

When someone spots a bird, point it out—again, quietly—and try to snag a zoomed-in photo. (It doesn't have to be perfect, just enough to help with identification.) Then record what kind of birds they are, if you recognize them, how many birds you spotted, and what they were doing. If you don't recognize a bird and didn't get a picture of it, sketch out a quick drawing or make notes about its appearance, color, and size. Then you can check a field guide or photos online to try to identify it.

BIRD CALLS

You may hear a bird without seeing it; this will happen more than you'd think. If you recognize the call, mark it down and add it to your count. If you don't know the call (again, this will happen pretty often), head online to a website like **All About Birds** (www.allaboutbirds.org), and listen to recordings of birds that could help you figure it out.

RECORD YOUR FINDS

After you're done counting birds for 15 minutes, combine all of your finds into a list. Consider setting up an account on a community science site such as **eBird** (www.ebird.org). There, you can create a "life list" of species spotted over time, and you'll also contribute to science—the resulting maps help create a snapshot of birdlife over time.

DO A BACKYARD BIRD COUNT

THE CHRISTMAS BIRD COUNT

Once you get the hang of doing a bird count, consider participating in a national one. There are two long-running bird counts. One is The Christmas Bird Count, which has been around for 120 years. It takes place from mid-December to early January, and volunteers spread out to count birds in specific areas around each state and the country, with counts occurring in each local area for only one day. Christmas Bird Counts are often an adventure that lasts several hours, so if you want to join in on the fun, tell your parents and prepare ahead of time! To find out more, visit www.audubon.org/conservation/science/christmas-bird-count.

THE GREAT BACKYARD BIRD COUNT

This bird count is similar to the Christmas Bird Count, but The Great Backyard Bird Count happens everywhere on the same dates in February. You can participate if you spot birds for as little as 15 minutes, making it easy to join. For more information and to sign up, visit www.birdcount.org.

Keep track of the birds you see or spot here!

PLANT A HUMMINGBIRD, BEE & BUTTERFLY GARDEN

One way you can help wildlife wherever you live is by making your area a bit wilder. The easiest way to do that is to plant native plants. You don't need a huge amount of space to do this; even a small container with native plants can help attract—and feed—pollinators.

WHAT TO DO

Here are a few examples of how to attract some of the more sought-after pollinators:

- Common sunflowers are easy to grow (sometimes they grow themselves when birds drop seeds), and they attract bumblebees, flies, and colorful beetles.

- Planting milkweed (such as Common Milkweed, Butterfly Milkweed, Swamp Milkweed) attracts Monarch Butterflies. The females lay their eggs on the plant, and the caterpillars munch away on the milkweed (they can be spotted if you take a close look).

- Plants with long tubular flowers, such as Coral Honeysuckle, attract hummingbirds and sphinx moths (large moths sometimes mistaken for hummingbirds).

Let the "weeds" be: Dandelions and plants like Carolina Clover provide bees, butterflies, and other beneficial insects with needed resources. Plus, not only are these plants pretty and great to walk on (clover doesn't get crunchy like turfgrass does), but they're tough and easy to care for.

For a dedicated list, see this excellent write-up at the website for the Xerces Society: www.xerces.org/pollinator-conservation/pollinator-friendly-plant-lists.

Once you plant your hummingbird, bee, and butterfly garden, keep track of the insects and birds you spot here.

_____

_____

_____

_____

_____

SET UP A WINDOW FEEDER

If you want to get an up-close look at birds, put up a window feeder. These transparent ledge-style feeders attach to a window with suction cups, and once the birds get used to the feeder and your presence on the other side of the glass, birds will chow down, enabling you to watch them from almost no distance at all.

BIRD NEST CAMS

For a different kind of up-close look at birds, head online and look at the many different nest cams offered on various bird sites. There are online nest cams for eagles hawks, ospreys, even hummingbirds.

For a list, visit www.allaboutbirds.org/cams.

MAKE YOUR WINDOWS SAFER FOR BIRDS

Hundreds of millions of birds are killed or injured each year when they accidentally fly into windows, often because they saw a reflection of nearby plants or the sky and thought it was a safe place to fly. Such collisions are often deadly, and they are a constant problem.

WHAT TO DO

There are a few simple steps you can take to help:

1. Close your blinds or curtains—this will make the window look more like a barrier. This is very important at night, when a lit-up room might seem like a welcoming place for a bird to fly.

2. When placing bird feeders, either keep them far away from windows (more than 20 feet) or keep them very close to windows—either directly on the window, using suction cups, or just a few feet away. (Even if a bird flies into a window from a close-by feeder, it won't fly fast enough to get seriously hurt.)

3. "Scare tape" or "flash tape"—reflective ribbons in iridescent colors that birds find scary looking—can be effective in keeping birds away from your windows.

4. Placing ribbons, pinwheels, and other moving accessories in front of windows can also scare birds away.

5. Keep plants away from windows, as birds often mistake them for part of the natural scenery outdoors.

WILDLIFE REHABILITATION NEAR YOU

If you see an animal get hurt or find one that you know is injured, contact your local wildlife rehabilitation center or a permit-carrying wildlife rehabilitation expert. To find one, check the website for your state's department of natural resources or department of fish and wildlife. (This department is named something slightly different depending on the state, so you may have to use different search terms.)

WHAT TO DO

If you find what you think is an orphaned baby animal and it's in a safe spot, don't pick it up. Instead, call your local wildlife rehabilitation center first—the animal actually might not be orphaned at all (its parents may be nearby or gathering food), and handling or disturbing the animal might actually do more harm than good. When in doubt, just leave the animal alone and call an expert.

Baby birds often fall out of nests, but they can usually be left for their parents to rescue. If you have a dog or a cat, though, check to make sure it's not roaming around outside.

Have you ever encountered an injured animal? What happened to it? Were you able to help it? Write your story here.

_____

_____

_____

_____

_____

_____

_____

_____

_____

_____

_____

_____

_____

_____

ASSEMBLING A COLLECTION OF STATE MINERALS & GEMS

Like state birds or state flowers, most states in the South have state gems, minerals, rocks, or fossils, but you may not have heard or know about all of them. Still, state rocks and minerals are almost always selected for their long history in the state, their economic impact, their beauty, or all of these things. Better yet, many of these state gems, minerals and fossils are easy to collect!

Important Note: Before you go out collecting, make sure it's allowed where you're looking for rocks. Don't go onto private property when collecting—that's against the law. In many cases, there are public places where you can legally collect rocks, though it might take some homework first!

And when it comes to vertebrate fossils (those with a backbone), collecting them is illegal unless you're a scientist. But you can still see them in person (at a museum, for example), or you can record them with a photo or drawing.

QUICK DEFINITION

A **mineral** usually consists of a combination of **chemical elements.** For example, table salt is a mineral (halite) made of two elements: sodium and chlorine. Sometimes, a single chemical element (like gold or silver) can be found in nature; those are considered minerals too. A **rock** is a combination of at least two minerals.

ALABAMA

RED IRON ORE

Iron ore has been mined for many years in Alabama—375 million tons have been extracted from the ground here since the nineteenth century.

MARBLE

Sylacauga marble is prized for its super-white color. It is a very popular stone worldwide thanks to its use in sculptures and as a building material. For example, the ceiling of the of Lincoln Memorial incorporates Sylacauga marble, as does the bust of Abraham Lincoln in the U.S. Capitol rotunda.

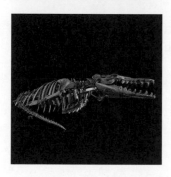

BASILOSAURUS CETOIDES

Do you have nightmares about giant sea creatures? This fossil whale could be the cause! *Basilosaurus cetoides* was an ancient species that lived 35–40 million years ago. They could grow 70 feet long, and they looked like a cross between a shark and a cow. You can't collect the fossils, but you can see a replica at the **Alabama Museum of Natural History** in Tuscaloosa (almnh.museums.ua.edu).

ASSEMBLING A COLLECTION OF STATE MINERALS & GEMS

MISSISSIPPI

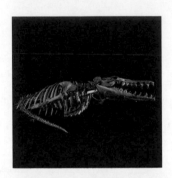

PREHISTORIC WHALE

In 1971 the nearly complete skeleton of a prehistoric whale was discovered near Tinsley, Mississippi, capturing attention statewide. In fact, two different ancient whale species called Mississippi home around 35-40 million years ago, when it was covered in water: *Basilosaurus cetoides* (shown here) and the similar but smaller *Zygorhiza kochii,* the prehistoric whale mentioned above, which was named Mississippi's state fossil in 1981.

PETRIFIED WOOD

Though it is the state stone, petrified wood is actually a fossil. Native Americans used the material to create tools, and the wood has been found across the state.

TEXAS

TEXAS BLUE TOPAZ

Though topaz is not commercially mined in Texas, enthusiasts and visitors can pan for topaz just like gold! Reach out to your local rock-collecting group to find out more.

TEXAS, *CONTINUED*

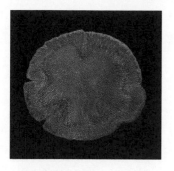

PETRIFIED PALMWOOD

Found in the eastern part of Texas, these fossils formed between 33 and 23 million years ago. The outside of the fossil often looks like vertical grooves, and the inside contains a spotted pattern. The type of palm that makes up this petrified wood is now extinct.

LOUISIANA

PETRIFIED PALMWOOD

Millions of years ago, the area we now know as Louisiana was a tropical ecosystem full of swaying palm trees. If they fell in mud or sediment and were covered up, these trees formed petrified palmwood! It comes in a multitude of colors and became Louisiana's state fossil in 1976.

CABOCHON-CUT OYSTER SHELL (LAPEARLITE)

Louisiana is known for its oysters, a type of shellfish found along the Gulf Coast. An individual oyster can filter up to 50 gallons of water each and every day. When specially cut and carefully polished, the oyster shells shine like pearls. The Eastern oyster (*Crassostrea virginica*) is the species used to make what is now Louisiana's state gemstone.

AGATE

While agate was once known as Louisiana's state gemstone, it was reclassified as the state mineral in the 21st century. Agate is known for its beautiful rings. Do you want to find agate of your own? Check out the Amite River!

ASSEMBLING A COLLECTION OF STATE MINERALS & GEMS

OKLAHOMA

BARITE ROSE (ROSE ROCK)

Formed from a combination of sand and barite, this rock looks like the petals of a fully opened rose. Rose rock can have as many as 20 "petals." Formed 250 million years ago when Oklahoma was covered with seawater, the water itself was integral in the rock creation.

SAUROPHAGANAX MAXIMUS

A giant, ferocious predator, *Saurophaganax maximus* once hunted in what is now Oklahoma. It lived more than 145 million years ago and could reach nearly 10,000 pounds. You can't collect the fossils, but you can see one up close at the **Sam Noble Oklahoma Museum of Natural History** in Norman (samnoblemuseum.ou.edu).

FLORIDA

AGATIZED CORAL

Though it looks like a rock, living coral is actually made up of thousands of tiny organisms, working together and creating critical habitat for a range of species. Over a period of 20-30 million years, the corals were replaced by a type of quartz called **chalcedony,** which retains the shape of the original coral. Today, agatized coral can be found in Tampa Bay, the Withlacoochee and Suwanee Rivers, and the Econfina River area.

MOONSTONE

Though not actually found in Florida, the moonstone was adopted as the official state gem of the Sunshine State in honor of the many space flights launched from the Kennedy Space Center in Brevard County. The moonstone is not found on the moon either, though: this gem naturally occurs in Pennsylvania and Virginia.

ARKANSAS

DIAMOND

At **Crater of Diamonds State Park** in Murfreesboro (tinyurl.com/crater ofdiamondsstatepark), you can not only hunt for diamonds, you can keep the ones you find! Since 1972, more than 33,000 diamonds have been discovered here. One, in fact, called Uncle Sam, is the largest diamond ever found in the U.S., weighing in at more than 40 carats!

Diamonds were formed billions of years ago when intense heat and pressure on carbon caused it to form crystals.

QUARTZ

Native Americans used quartz to tip their tools and hunting gear. Commercial quartz mining in Arkansas began in the nineteenth century. The quality of quartz in this region is particularly high, drawing both scientists and amateur rock collectors from around the world.

ASSEMBLING A COLLECTION OF STATE MINERALS & GEMS

SOUTH CAROLINA

AMETHYST

Named as the state gem in 1969, amethyst is actually a form of colored quartz. Known for its purple color, amethyst can be dark hued or much lighter. Did you know that you can find amethyst in South Carolina?

BLUE GRANITE

If you build with granite in the United States, it could come from South Carolina! Named the state stone in 1969, blue granite is known for the color shade it takes on when polished. Builders used blue granite when constructing the South Carolina Statehouse.

COLUMBIAN MAMMOTH

In the eighteenth century, enslaved South Carolina plantation workers discovered the fossilized teeth of a mammoth in a swamp. The Columbian Mammoth became the state fossil in 2014 after a third-grader who loves science and history wrote to her senator suggesting the inclusion of the large, extinct mammal as an official South Carolina symbol. You can't collect this fossil, but you can see a display about it at the **South Carolina State Museum** in Columbia (scmuseum.org).

NORTH CAROLINA

MEGALODON SHARK TEETH

The North Carolina coast boasts one of the largest collections of *Megalodon* teeth in the world. They are more common off the coast, in deep tracts that were once riverbeds. Some teeth can be six inches in length—now that is a *big* tooth! *Megalodon* was a huge shark that became extinct about 3.6 million years ago.

GOLD

In 1799 European settlers discovered gold in North Carolina, and until 1828 it was the only state that produced gold. In fact, until gold was discovered in California in 1848, most of America's gold came from North Carolina. Today you won't find it here in large amounts, but many visitors and locals alike enjoy panning for gold recreationally.

GRANITE

Granite has been mined in North Carolina since 1805. It's an igneous rock, made up of quartz, alkali feldspar, and plagioclase.

ASSEMBLING A COLLECTION OF STATE MINERALS & GEMS

VIRGINIA

CHESAPECTEN JEFFERSONIUS

A fossilized scallop shell, this unique formation was designated as an official state symbol in 1993. It was the first fossil from North America to be described by Europeans in the seventeenth century. These scallops lived 4–5 million years ago. These fossils can be found in a number of places in Virginia; join a local rock and mineral club to find out where to look!

NELSONITE

Dark with white speckles, nelsonite was named Virginia's official state rock in 2016. An igneous rock, nelsonite is made up primarily of ilmenite and apatite, and it's a good source of titanium (a useful metal) and calcium phosphate (used to make fertilizer).

WEST VIRGINIA

SILICIFIED MISSISSIPPIAN FOSSIL CORAL (*LITHOSTROTIONELLA*)

Around 350–325 million years ago, water covered much of North America, providing ample habitat for the coral that now makes up West Virginia's state gem. It is a popular material for making jewelry.

TENNESSEE

PTEROTRIGONIA THORACICA

A fossilized shell, this pretty bivalve displays raised ridges. About 70 million years ago, it buried itself in the sediment and filtered water to find food. This species is now extinct.

TENNESSEE PEARLS

Though they form only rarely in nature, Tennessee river pearls are now farmed from native freshwater mussels. Pearls are formed when grains of sand enter into the soft insides of a mussel, and they create the pearly layers (or **nacre**) to stop the irritation.

AGATE

With gorgeous, undulating colors, this particular type of agate (a form of the mineral quartz) is found in only a few parts of Tennessee.

LIMESTONE

Made up of calcium carbonate, limestone is a popular building material. It forms when sediment, especially coral skeletons and algae, hardens into layers over time.

ASSEMBLING A COLLECTION OF STATE MINERALS & GEMS

KENTUCKY

BRACHIOPOD

Brachiopod shells are the most common fossils in Kentucky. To gather food, brachiopods took in water between their open shells, filtered it for edible particles, and then whooshed the water back out again.

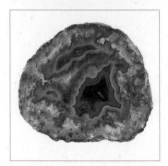

KENTUCKY AGATE

Though it is the official state rock, agate is not a rock at all. Kentucky agate is a form of mineral quartz. The agate contains many layered colors, which is usually a result of other chemicals, like iron or calcium.

FRESHWATER PEARL

Though gemstones are usually minerals, the freshwater pearl is formed when irritants like sand are inserted (either in nature or through farming) into freshwater mussels. The mussels create the pearl in order to relieve themselves of the irritating sand! Mussels spend two to three years forming pearls, which have been prized as jewels for centuries.

COAL

Millions of years ago, dead plants turned into peat. When this layer was buried over time, the heat and pressure of the earth's crust converted the peat to coal, which has been mined as a source of energy for hundreds of years. Unfortunately, burning coal releases carbon dioxide into the atmosphere, where it contributes to climate change.

Note: State symbols are approved by each state's **legislature** (the elected officials who make laws), so not every state has approved the same categories. That's why some states have more symbols than others, and why the same symbol may be worded differently from state to state (for instance, *gem* instead of *gemstone*).

QUICK QUIZ

What is the difference between a rock and a mineral?

_____

_____

_____

Answer on page 147!

TESTING THE HARDNESS OF MINERALS

Hardness is a useful way to help identify your mineral finds. The **Mohs Hardness Scale**, on the right, ranks some common minerals in terms of hardness, or how easily they can be scratched. Talc, the lowest mineral on the scale, is so soft you can scratch it with your fingers. Diamond is famous for being one of the hardest minerals, and for good reason: almost no natural substances can scratch it.

Making your own hardness test kit is a good way to start learning hands-on with rocks and minerals. Determining a mineral's hardness is a good first step in trying to identify it.

The way the scale works is simple: any material lower on the scale can be scratched by materials above it. So gypsum can scratch talc, but talc can't scratch gypsum. Similarly, calcite, which is a 3, can scratch gypsum *and* talc.

WHAT YOU'LL NEED

Using the scale to test your finds usually goes like this: You find a mineral (not a rock!) and you're not sure what it is. You start out by trying to scratch it with your fingernail. If it leaves a scratch, then it's softer than 2.5 on the scale. Chances are, however, it won't leave a scratch. So you need to move up to a different piece of equipment with a known hardness.

Here are some common, easy-to-find examples:

• Fingernail: 2.5

• A real piece of copper (not a penny, as these coins aren't made of much copper anymore): 3

• Steel nail or a knife: 5.5–6 (for safety reasons, you should have an adult help you with these tests)

• A piece of quartz: 7

Talc
$Mg_3Si_4O_{10}(OH)_2$

Gypsum
$CaSO_4 \cdot 2H_2O$

Calcite
$CaCO_3$

Fluorite
CaF_2

Apatite
$Ca_5(PO_4)_3(F,Cl,OH)$

WHAT TO DO

To scratch it, you need to hold the to-be-scratched mineral firmly in one hand, and use a pointed area of the "scratching" mineral and press firmly, away from your body or fingers. If it leaves a scratch mark, it's softer than the "scratching" mineral. Obviously, for safety reasons you should make sure you have an adult conduct the actual scratch tests—don't handle a knife or a nail yourself.

Once you've found something that scratches it, you're pretty close to figuring out its hardness. Then it's just a matter of scratching it with other minerals from the chart or your scratching tools, then seeing if you can figure out an even more specific range. Once you've narrowed down the hardness some more, looking up mineral hardness is easy online.

Note: You can also buy lab-calibrated "hardness pick" kits; these are much more accurate, but they can be expensive.

Keep track of your hardness tests here. Doing so can help you learn to identify your finds!

Orthoclase
$KAlSi_3O_8$

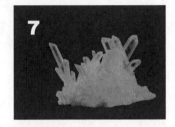

Quartz
SiO_2

Topaz
$Al_2SiO_4(F,OH)_2$

Corundum
Al_2O_3

Diamond
C

LOOKING AT SOIL, DIRT, OR A DEAD LOG

Rocks and minerals are definitely showier than plain old dirt or soil, but that's only until you get an up-close look. Once you do, with a magnifying glass, a macro camera, or a small microscope, you'll be surprised at what you find.

WHAT TO DO

Roll over a dead log and strip off a piece of bark. A dead log might look, well, dead, but it's actually its own little world. Insects, such as wasps, burrow into the wood to lay their eggs. Under the bark, ants and beetles are busy tunneling or making a home (they often leave behind intricate patterns on the wood). And it's easy to spot tiny mushrooms and sometimes very colorful slime molds, which are often food sources for other animals, such as slugs, snails, and insects.

Safety Note: If you have venomous spiders or snakes in your area, make sure you go out with an adult and take proper precautions (wear gloves, long pants, and so on) when digging in dirt or turning over logs.

WHAT YOU MIGHT SEE

• Slugs or tiny land snails

• Lichen (an organism that consists of algae and/or bacteria and fungi, living together)

• Slime molds

• Spiders, ants, tiny insects, and other animals

QUICK QUESTIONS

1. How many types of life did you find?

_____

_____

2. Were you able to identify them all?

_____

_____

MAKE A CAST OF AN ANIMAL TRACK

You might think that animal tracks won't last very long, but that's not always true. You can actually preserve a track using plaster. Follow the instructions below to make your very own track cast!

WHAT YOU'LL NEED

• A strip of plastic or cardboard long enough to wrap around your track

• A paper clip

• Plaster of Paris

• A container for mixing

WHAT TO DO

1. Remove any twigs or leaves around the track.

2. Use the plastic or cardboard to create a "wall" around the track. Use the paper clip to secure the ends together.

3. Add two parts dry plaster for every one part water (so if you use 1 cup of dry plaster, you should use $1/2$ cup of water).

4. Mix the plaster and water together until it's like pancake batter. Stir until the plaster isn't lumpy, usually at least a few minutes.

5. Pour the plaster inside your wall (but not directly onto the track), letting the plaster flow over the track gradually. Pour enough to cover the entire track to a depth of about $3/4$ inch.

6. Wait half an hour, then test the firmness of the plaster. Once it's hard enough, remove it by grabbing it at the edges. Wait a few days for it to dry completely, and you then can frame it or put it on display.

Have an adult help you when creating a cast, as it can be a bit tricky. Once you have a cast, you can even frame it.

MAKE A SELF-PORTRAIT USING NATURE

WHAT YOU'LL NEED

• Several blank pieces of paper

• A glue stick, if you want to create a permanent piece of art

WHAT TO DO

With an adult, start out by gathering some twigs; these are a great way to create a general outline of your face. Then start thinking about the color of your skin, hair, and eyes, and look around for natural objects that are a close match. It's best to choose from things that you know are safe to touch: rocks and pebbles, sand, dandelions, flower petals, oaks, maples, grass, moss, tree bark, and so on. If you're not sure if you can touch it, leave it alone or ask an adult. That way, you can avoid Poison Ivy, Poison Oak, Poison Sumac, and anything icky.

When you're done, take a picture of your portrait; then put your natural parts back where you found them, and your paper in the recycling or trash. If you want to keep the portrait, you can glue each object to the paper and then frame it. Just make sure no little kids have access to the actual leaves and flowers and such.

GEOLOGY & GEMSTONES CROSSWORD

ACROSS

3. What state rock looks like the petals of a flower?

4. Visitors can search for this state gemstone in creekbeds and ravines.

5. What is a state mineral, but can also be burned for fuel?

7. The state gem of Tennessee and Kentucky, these form inside freshwater mussel shells.

10. A popular building material.

11. This sparkly state gem is used in jewelry.

DOWN

1. What is the second-most abundant mineral on earth?

2. What has been chosen as an official state rock, though it is not a rock at all?

6. Virginia's state rock.

8. Yellow, shiny, and used for money and jewelry, this is the state mineral of North Carolina.

9. State mineral mined from Alabama.

Answers on page 148!

Hint: One of the answers is pictured here.

LEARNING TO IDENTIFY
BASIC GROUPS OF BUGS

If you want to learn about insects, start by learning to identify the basic groups (or orders) of insects. Some, such as butterflies and moths, you might already know, but there are quite a few more to discover. This list isn't all-inclusive, but it gives you a fun idea of some of the insects you can find!

ANTS, BEES AND WASPS (*HYMENOPTERA*)

Honeybee

Bumblebee

Metallic Green Sweat Bee

Tricolored Bee

Carpenter Ant

Yellowjacket

Long-Tailed Ichneumon Wasp

BUTTERFLIES & MOTHS (*LEPIDOPTERA*)

White-Lined
Sphinx Moth

Io Moth

Monarch Butterfly

Zebra Longwing

FLIES (*DIPTERA*)

House Fly

Robber Fly

Mosquito

Margined
Calligrapher Fly

LEARNING TO IDENTIFY
BASIC GROUPS OF BUGS

BEETLES (*COLEOPTERA*)

Spotted Cucumber Beetle

Convergent Ladybug

Colorado Potato Beetle

Goldenrod Soldier Beetle

Big Dipper Firefly

Reddish-Brown Stag Beetle

Green June Bug

Whirligig Beetles

MAYFLIES (*EPHEMEROPTERA*)

White Burrower Flathead

Blue-Winged Olive Mayfly

Epeorus Mayfly

TRUE BUGS (*HEMIPTERA*)

Milkweed
Assassin Bug

Cicada

Candy-Striped
Leafhopper

Giant Water Bug

DAMSELFLIES & DRAGONFLIES (*ODONATA*)

Regal Darner
Dragonfly

Ebony Jewelwing

Eastern
Amberwing

Great Pondhawk

SPIDERS (*ARANEAE*)

Wolf Spider

Banana Spider

Green Lynx Spider

Yellow Garden
Spider

LEARNING TO IDENTIFY
BASIC GROUPS OF BUGS

NON-INSECTS

Centipede

Millipede

Isopod

Earthworm

BUGS TO AVOID

Deer Tick

Mosquito

In which month do you see the most insects where you live?

_____

_____

_____

MAKE YOUR YARD
A LITTLE WILDER

Many insect populations are at risk. Habitat destruction, insecticide spraying (which kills a lot more than just mosquitoes), and water pollution can all play a role. Lawns, in particular, are part of the problem, as they are incredibly widespread and not all that useful for many plants and animals. That's why it's helpful to make your yard a bit wilder.

WHAT TO DO

With your parents' OK, make a portion of your yard a little bit more like nature. Plant a mix of native flowering plants there, don't spray insecticides or herbicides in that area or mow it as heavily, and leave out some deadwood for insect habitat. Then, over time, keep track of the critters you find, and compare it to the rest of your yard. You'll find that even a small patch of plants can attract critters you may have never seen before.

Before you create a "wild patch" of your yard, write down your plan below. What are you hoping to attract?

_____

_____

_____

_____

RAISE NATIVE CATERPILLARS & RELEASE THEM

Finding a caterpillar is one of the highlights of spring and summer. But unless it's a really well-known caterpillar, like a Monarch, identifying caterpillars can be tricky for beginners. Many caterpillars, including all of the classic inchworms, will actually end up being moths. Even the name scientists use for these moths—Geometridae—is a reference to geometry and how these caterpillars "measure" as they walk.

But you don't need to identify your caterpillar to rear it; after all, one of the most fun ways to identify a moth or a butterfly is after it's turned into an adult!

WHAT YOU'LL NEED

• A butterfly house (it's best to purchase a high-quality one online first)

• An ample supply of fresh leaves

• A water source for the leaves, but one that the caterpillar can't enter (pill bottles work great)

WHAT TO DO

When you find a caterpillar, immediately note what plant you find it on, and if it's on the ground, the plants that are nearby. These are likely the caterpillar's host plants (the ones it needs to eat to become an adult). If you're unsure of which plants to gather, bring in a sampling of several different kinds. If you want an exact answer, post a photo of your caterpillar on a site like BugGuide.net and ask for help on finding out what it eats.

Once you have the caterpillar and the host plants, you'll need to ready your butterfly house. Many common commercially available houses are mesh cylinders.

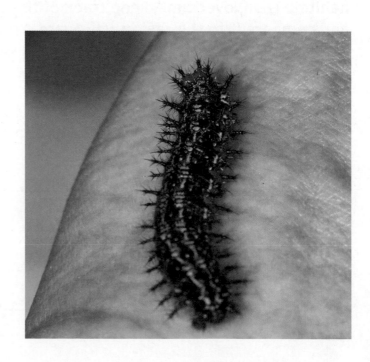

First, prepare your water source for the host plants. Do not provide a water dish or another water source at the bottom of a butterfly house; caterpillars drown easily. Instead, have a parent help you drill or cut a hole in a small container, like an old pill bottle, and put the plant stems into the water source (but make sure the caterpillar can't fall into the water and drown).

Over time, you'll need to replace the leaves and clean up its poop (known as frass). Eventually, the caterpillar will begin to pupate. This is a fascinating process in its own right, but watching one emerge is even better.

Of course, things can go wrong when collecting wild caterpillars: Parasitic wasps often attack or infest caterpillars; if your cage is dirty, they can get sick; and if you find a caterpillar in late summer, it might be one that spends the winter as a pupa. Still, with practice, there's a good chance that you'll get to watch moths and butterflies all summer long if you work at it hard enough!

Note: It's best to only collect smooth or slightly bumpy caterpillars—those with fuzz or hairs may make you itchy if you touch them.

GET TO KNOW THE SOUTH'S NATIVE BEES

If you've been following the news, you know that bee populations are in trouble. But you're probably most familiar with honeybees, which are actually an introduced species native to Europe, not the U.S. Think of honeybees as farm animals. The honeybees you see in your yard? In a sense, those are kind of like escaped chickens or cows.

Domesticated honeybee populations have run into trouble over the past few decades due to a combination of factors, including pests (especially the Varroa mite), pesticide use, and habitat loss. These domesticated insects play a critical role in pollinating agricultural crops, especially almonds, blueberries, and cherries.

Honeybees aren't the only bees in the U.S. that are threatened, however; on the contrary, while honeybees get much of the press, there are thousands of native bee species in the U.S., and many of them are threatened or imperiled due to habitat loss, loss of suitable nesting sites, and the like. They range from the

QUICK QUIZ

Which one of these is a bee?

1. _____ 2. _____ 3. _____

Answers on page 147!

familiar bumblebees that flutter along your flowers to carpenter bees, which bore into wood.

The South hosts many native bees, including: Sweat Bees, Rusty-Patched Bumblebees, Southeastern Blueberry Bees, Blue Orchard Mason Bees, Two-Spotted Long-Horned Bees, and more.

BEES

Sweat Bee

Southeastern Blueberry Bee

Rusty-Patched Bumblebee

Mason Bee

Two-Spotted Long-Horned Bee

BEE LOOK-ALIKES

Yellow Fly (watch out, it bites!)

Locust Borer Beetle

START AN INSECT COLLECTION

If you love bugs, creating a bug collection can help you observe them up close, but if you're not into killing bugs, there's another option. When you're out in nature, chances are you'll notice dead insects if you're paying attention. If a bug is dead but in reasonably good shape, you can add it to your collection. You'll be surprised at what you find: butterflies and moths, gorgeous beetles, and so on (after all, insects don't live very long).

One of the easiest ways to store insects is with a Riker Mount, a simple glass case with padding that holds the insects against the glass.

OPTIONAL PROJECT

If you want to collect live samples, placing them in a zip-top plastic bag and freezing them is one way to kill them humanely. On sites like BugGuide.net, you can also look up "killing jars" online that use common household chemicals.

What is your favorite type of insect? Why?

_____

_____

_____

_____

_____

_____

MAKE AN ULTRAVIOLET BUG TRAP

Have you ever noticed how bugs are attracted to lights at night? This happens because nocturnal insects use light to navigate, and artificial lights confuse them. With a simple setup, you can set up your own "light trap" to attract bugs. It's a wonderful way to see insects you might not otherwise see.

WHAT YOU'LL NEED

- A lantern, an ultraviolet lamp. or a blacklight (available online)

- An extension cord

- An old bedsheet or a curtain (light-colored ones are best)

- Two sections of rope

- A pair of scissors

- Flashlights

- A camera

WHAT TO DO

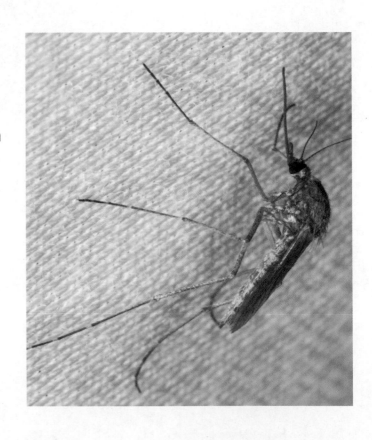

With an adult supervising, cut holes in the corners at one end of the bedsheet, and have the adult help you tie a section of rope to each hole in the bedsheet or curtain. (Curtains often have ready-made loops that make things easier.)

Then look for a good spot to find bugs; generally, the wilder it is, the better, but you'll need to be within reach of an outdoor-safe extension cord so you can plug in your light. Near woods, bushes, or other plants is good, but even the middle of a suburban yard will have all sorts of bugs you've likely never seen.

Tie one rope to a tree branch, a bird feeder hook, or another support, then pull the rope on the other side of the curtain until the whole thing is taut, hanging like a movie screen. Tie the bottom to a chair or anything else heavy enough to hold it. About an hour before sundown, find a chair and place it on either side of the curtain, set your light on it, and plug it into the extension cord, shining it onto the curtain (but not close enough to touch it).

Then wait and make periodic visits to the sheet to see what you find! Heading out with a flashlight in one hand and a camera in another is an easy way to record your finds (and identify them later on).

Once you get a look at the insects you've attracted, wait a while longer and visit again later in the night (some of the best bug hunting is late at night)

Note: When you are observing moths, the light might shine on you and your clothes a bit, so it's possible (though not all that likely) to have moths or other bugs land on you. To avoid this, wear a dark shirt (not one that matches the "moth sheet"). A few bugs may land on you, but gently brushing them off with a stick or a gloved hand is enough to make them fly away.

CRICKET MATH

Crickets are famously noisy insects; the males rub their front wings (not their legs!) together to attract females. That much you probably knew. But did you know that you can count a cricket's chirps to tell the approximate temperature outside?

The math is simple: Go outside and listen for a cricket that's chirping. Count the number of its chirps for 13 seconds, then add 40 to that total. Then check it against the temperature for your area: to find that, go to www.noaa.gov and look for your local weather in the top-right corner.

Pretty wild, right? Try it again on a different day and record your findings below.

The reason this works out is actually relatively simple: Crickets, like all insects, are cold-blooded, so their body temperature depends on the surrounding air. So when it's warmer, their metabolism speeds up, and so do the chirps! When it's colder, their chirps slow down.

Number of chirps in 13 seconds _____ + 40 = _____

Number of chirps in 13 seconds _____ + 40 = _____

Number of chirps in 13 seconds _____ + 40 = _____

Number of chirps in 13 seconds _____ + 40 = _____

Number of chirps in 13 seconds _____ + 40 = _____

Original research by Dr. Peggy LeMone and James Larsen:
www.questia.com/library/journal/1G1-272666064/the-sound-of-crickets-using-evidence-based-reasoning

BUGS & INSECTS CROSSWORD

ACROSS

1. This insect is very important for many farmers, as it helps pollinate their crops, but it's not native to the South.

4. The word for a larval (juvenile) moth or butterfly.

6. Butterflies usually fly during the day; this group of related insects look similar, but most (but not all) fly at night.

8. This animal isn't an insect at all; robins love to eat them.

DOWN

2. This group of insects has a hard outer covering on their wings. Ladybugs and June bugs belong to this group.

3. This insect is famous for chirping at night, and if you count its chirps over 13 seconds, you can even use it as a thermometer!

5. These beautiful, fast-flying insects love to zoom around in summer, snatching bugs in midair.

7. This group of caterpillars is known to scientists as the geometers, but most people call them this, for the way they seem to "measure out" distance as they walk along.

9. There are many different kinds of this red, spotted insect.

Answers on page 148!

START LOOKING AT MUSHROOMS

When you think of mushrooms, you might think of the red-and-white mushrooms from *Super Mario Brothers* or the familiar white mushrooms sold at the grocery store. They are only two types of fungi, and scientists think there may be millions of species in the world, most of which scientists don't know much, if anything, about. The South alone is probably home to thousands of species of fungi. Some have a **mutualistic** (equally beneficial) relationship with trees, helping them get nutrients.

Others are **saprobes** (they consume dead or dying trees or other natural materials). Still others are microscopic but very important, such as the yeast (a fungus!) that helps make the bread in your peanut-butter-and-jelly sandwich.

In the South, mushrooms can be classified in a few simple ways. Obviously, this list is not all-inclusive, and it's no replacement for a field guide (or five!), but these general categories are helpful to know.

Important Note: Do **not** eat wild mushrooms. Some are very **toxic** (poisonous) to eat and tricky to identify. Wait until you're older and have trained, experienced adults to help you out.

You can touch them safely (even the toxic ones), but just in case, wear gloves. And if you're making a spore print (see page 122) or a sketch, do that outside. Throw the mushrooms in the garbage when you're done.

See page 119 for our tips on spotting mushrooms.

CAP AND STEM WITH GILLS

Mushrooms with a stem and a cap, with gills underneath.

Peach Fly Agaric

Unidentified Find

Green-Spored Lepiota

Amethyst Laccaria

Marasmius

CAP AND STEM WITH PORES

Mushrooms with a cap and a stem, but with tiny holes (pores) underneath.

Ash Bolete

Ash Bolete (underside)

Scaber Stalk

START LOOKING AT MUSHROOMS

SHELF MUSHROOMS

Mushrooms that mostly grow out from trees, like a shelf; they can have pores or gills.

Chicken of the Woods

Artist's Conk

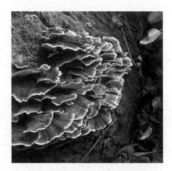

A bracket fungus

ROUND MUSHROOMS

Mushrooms that grow on the ground, in a ball or oval-like shape. Some puffballs can get as large as a soccer ball, and they're famous for "popping" and releasing a cloud of spores. But don't breathe in the dust—it can make you sick.

Puffball

Earthball

Earthstar

SURPRISING MUSHROOMS

Mushrooms that are hard to describe because of their brain-like shapes or weird consistency.

Dead Man's Fingers

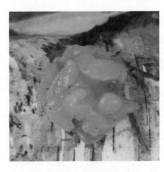

Witches' Butter

Wrinkled Peach

Coral Fungi

False Morel

TIPS FOR SPOTTING MUSHROOMS

- Look for mushrooms after a rain (they can pop up quite quickly).

- Look near the bases of dying trees or on dead logs.

- Mushrooms often seem to grow from the ground, but they might actually be growing from wood in the soil.

- Slime molds often grow under bark.

START LOOKING
AT MUSHROOMS

SLIME MOLDS

Slime molds were once considered fungi, but they're now classified differently. Still, they are often grouped together with fungi, so here are a few! They're really weird, and by the way, they can move—but slowly, so you need a time-lapse camera to see it.

Dog Vomit Slime
Mold (gross!)

Chocolate Tube
Slime Mold

Wolf's Milk
Slime Mold

1. Page through a field guide to mushrooms, then go and look for them in your area, especially if it has rained lately (mushrooms often spring up after rains). Jot down notes about them here! But remember: **Don't eat wild mushrooms.** Take notes and pictures instead!

_____

_____

_____

_____

_____

2. Sketch your mushroom finds here!

MAKE MUSHROOM SPORE PRINTS

Mushrooms reproduce via spores. Spores are too small to see individually without a microscope, but there's an easy and fun way to spot them: by making a spore print. For a number of technical reasons, spores aren't considered the same thing as a seed in a plant, but the basic idea is the same: spores help fungi reproduce. And they do that by leaving microscopic spores behind almost everywhere. Spore colors vary by species, and they can produce some neat results. To see for yourself, make a spore print.

WHAT YOU'LL NEED

• Small bowls or cups

• White paper and, if possible, some construction paper of various colors

• Different kinds of mushrooms, with cap and stems or cap and gills

WHAT TO DO

With a knife, cut off the cap of each mushroom—or take a good section of a shelf mushroom—and place it on top of a piece of paper. (The gills or pores should be facing down onto the paper.) Place a small bowl or a cup over each mushroom. Mushroom spore colors vary a lot, so it's helpful to change up the paper color; a mushroom with light-colored spores won't show up well on white paper, for instance. Wait an hour or so, remove the bowl, and throw the mushroom in the trash. Then admire the spore print left behind!

Important Note: Have an adult handle the knife, and don't make spore prints in your kitchen or another area where food is served, or where someone could mistake the mushrooms for food. A garage is a good place to make spore prints.

CARVE ARTIST'S CONK

Artist's Conk is a special kind of shelf mushroom that grows on dead or dying trees. At first glance, it doesn't look like much. It's pretty plain looking on the top—oval shaped and brown and white—and underneath it's just a drab white.

Artist's Conk gets its name because its white pores turn a dark brown when scratched. And the scratches then stay that way, making it a favorite of "scratch artists." This makes Artist's Conk something like nature's Etch A Sketch.

Of course, to identify Artist's Conk, you'll need an adult's help and a field guide, but it's not too tricky to spot once you start looking.

Note: Please only carve Artist's Conk that you have collected. Don't carve it if it's still in the woods.

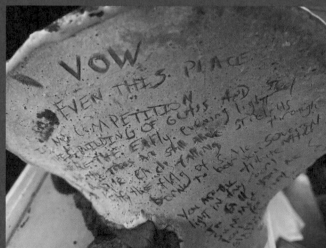

Before you carve your Artist's Conk, you might want to practice writing down your message here. When you're writing on a mushroom, you can't use an eraser, so practicing here first can help you get it right.

_____

_____

_____

_____

_____

_____

_____

_____

_____

_____

_____

_____

_____

SPOTTING THE MOON, THE PLANETS & ORION

In winter, it can be hard to stay active outside—after all, it's cooler out and it gets dark earlier. But for stargazers, winter is one of the best seasons around. In fact, some of the best constellations are visible during the winter. So if you dress up warmly, grab a lawn chair, and bust out a small telescope or binoculars, you can see the planets, the moon, or even the Orion Nebula and the Pleiades star cluster.

WHAT YOU'LL NEED

• Warm clothes

• A lawn chair

• A small telescope or, if you don't have one, binoculars

• A field guide and/or virtual planetarium software like **Stellarium** (which is free for Windows computers and Macs)

WHAT TO DO

First, figure out what you want to see before you head out. That's where a good field guide comes in. Virtual planetarium software is great, too, because it can show you exactly what the sky will look like wherever you are (and whenever you want).

Starting with the moon is always a good idea—it's bright and impossible to miss. when it's up. The best time to observe the moon is in its first quarter, when only one half of the moon is lit up—this reveals a lot more detail than a full moon, when all that reflected sunlight washes out the view. If you have a small telescope, try holding a smartphone over the eyepiece and see if you can snap some pictures. This can be tricky, but if you take a bunch of pictures and fiddle with the settings, you can get some wonderful shots. (There are also phone mounts you can buy fairly inexpensively online, but you have to be sure to get the right model for your phone.)

After you take a look at the moon, make sure you get a chance to see Jupiter, Saturn, Mars, and Venus. You'll need to refer to your field guide or planetarium software for when and where to look for each, because they appear to move through the sky over time. Still, it's worth the effort: seeing Saturn's rings for the first time will make you gasp.

Note: Don't expect to see the rings like you would in a picture from NASA—the planets will look pretty darn small. But if you're patient and you focus just right, you'll see the planets for real. It's an amazing experience. Even if you just have binoculars, you can often spot Jupiter's four largest moons: Io, Europa, Ganymede, and Callisto.

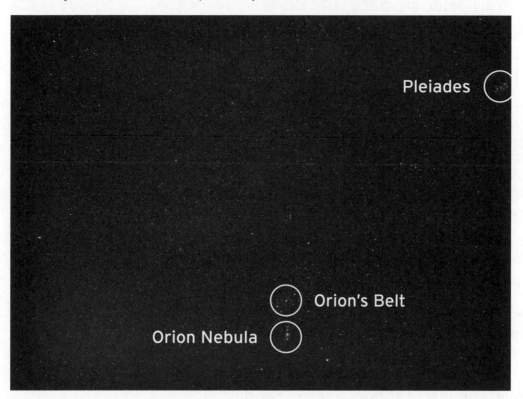

Finally, even if you only have a small telescope or binoculars, make sure to take a look at the constellation Orion. Easy to spot throughout much of the late fall and winter, it's famous for Orion's Belt, a line of three evenly spaced stars at the center of the constellation. If you look just below the belt, you'll see a star that looks a bit smudged; it's actually not a star at all. It's a **nebula,** or an area where stars are forming. Viewed through binoculars or a small telescope, it's a wonderful sight. The same is true for the Pleiades, a bright star cluster. To find it, simply follow from Orion's Belt up and to the right. If you're just looking with your eyes, it looks like a little smudge, but through binoculars or a telescope, it looks kind of like a miniature version of the Big Dipper.

SPOT THE INTERNATIONAL SPACE STATION (ISS)

If you really want an amazing sight, see if you can observe the International Space Station as it passes overhead. Continuously inhabited by astronauts since the year 2000, the International Space Station is massive—longer than football field—and its huge solar panels reflect a lot of light back to Earth. This makes it incredibly bright in the night sky as it passes overhead.

WHAT TO DO

To spot it, visit the excellent website **Spot the Station** (spotthestation.nasa.gov), and check the forecast for the next times the station will pass overhead at your location. It'll be visible either in the morning (sometimes quite early) or in the evening. But if you're patient, there are quite a few options, and you can make observing the ISS a fun habit. If you want a challenge, try snapping a photo of it as it passes overhead.

And once you spot it, you can visit the website www.howmany peopleareinspacerightnow.com to learn who was aboard the ISS as it flew by.

1. What was it like seeing the International Space Station?

_____

_____

2. How long did you see it, and how bright was it in the sky compared with the stars and planets?

_____

_____

International
Space Station

CONDUCT A BACKYARD BIO-BLITZ

A **bio-blitz** is an event where nature lovers—usually in a large group—try to record all of the life in a given area during a set period of time. But you don't need to be a scientist to do a bio-blitz; you can do one yourself or with your family. And you can do one wherever you are: in your backyard, on a trip, even from the window of a car or from an apartment balcony. The basic idea is simple: you want to try to identify as many life forms as you can within a certain amount of time.

WHAT YOU WILL NEED

- A magnifying glass

- A smartphone

- A notebook and pen for each person

- Field guides

WHAT TO DO

The simplest way to start off is in your backyard or a green space near where you live. Have an adult set a timer for 15 minutes. Start out with the easy stuff first: the grass, any weeds that you recognize (dandelions), and birds or mammals (such as chipmunks or squirrels). It's helpful to be systematic: start in one area, and look it over carefully before moving on to the next.

For each life form you find, write down what you think it is and where you found it. Take a picture, or draw it if you don't know what it is and want to look it up. See how many different kinds of animals and plants you can find and record them on the form to the right!

Bonus: If you can look it up, try to find the **scientific name** for what you found. Scientific names exist to make it easier for scientists to talk to each other clearly. For example, there are three main different kinds of bears in North America: Black Bears, Brown Bears, and Polar Bears. So the word *bear* isn't very specific. And for many creatures, including insects, there simply aren't any common names. A scientific name is a special name that has two parts: a **genus name,** which is like a last name and is shared with other similar animals, and a **species name**, which is like a first name. Together, that name is unique for that animal. For example, only one plant has the name *Taraxacum officinale*: the Common Dandelion, and scientists all over the world can refer to it, even if they don't speak the same language!

WHAT IS IT?	LOCATION	SCIENTIFIC NAME
Plants		
Dandelion	By the swing set	*Taraxacum officinale*
White Oak Tree	In the front yard	*Quercus alba*
Birds		
American Robin	On the White Oak Tree	*Turdus migratorius*
Mammals		
Gray Squirrel	?	
Insects		
Unidentified but Cool		

CONTRIBUTE TO A COMMUNITY SCIENCE PROJECT

iNATURALIST

If your parents have a smartphone, or you have one of your own, ask if it's OK to download **iNaturalist.** This app is all about nature. It's a wonderful way to keep track of and identify your finds, and you can help science in the process.

WHAT TO DO

The way it works is simple. You sign up (you have to be 13 years old to have your own account), and then you take a photo of an animal, plant, or mushroom that you spot. You then create an observation, add the photo, and click on the "What Did You See?" button. The app will run the photo through a computer program that will attempt to identify it; the program isn't perfect, but it often helps you narrow down what you found.

Then, if you share the observation and location online, other observers (including experts) can help confirm your identification (or propose a new one). Once an observation has two identifications that are the same, it's considered "research grade" and it can be used by scientists!

In fact, this might happen faster than you think. I've had several scientists contact me about my photos, either because the species hadn't been recorded in that area or because they wanted a sample of the species. In short, it's an easy way to do a little real science yourself.

Note: If you or your parents are concerned about your privacy (ask them if you're not sure), you don't have to post your exact location—there's an option to click "Obscured" under "Geolocation." This will keep people from seeing exactly where you made your observation and instead only gives a large range instead.

eBIRD

Do you love looking at birds? Recording your observations using **eBird** (ebird.org), a website and app created by the Cornell Lab of Ornithology. Scientists use observations gathered from birders around the world to learn more about where birds breed, migrate, and winter.

PROJECT BUDBURST

When do trees get their buds and leaves? When do flowers open their petals? When do marsh grasses change color? These observations are centered on a plant's phenology, and they tell us important information about the seasons. Contribute your observations to **Project BudBurst** (budburst .org), and help researchers learn about how climate change and other regional changes are affecting plants.

Keep track of your community science discoveries here by making a "life list" of the plants, animals, and fungi you've spotted.

_____

_____

_____

_____

_____

_____

NATURE BINGO

Circle the nature you see, and see who gets a bingo first!

NATURE

BINGO

DANDELION	LICHEN	MAMMAL	OAK LEAF	GRASS
CONIFEROUS TREE	ROCK	MOSS	DRAGONFLY	CLOUD
SPIDER	ANT	FREE THE SKY SPACE	BEETLE	DECIDUOUS TREE
THE MOON	WORM	BIRD	LOG	STAR (THE SUN COUNTS!)
MUSHROOM	MAPLE LEAF	PINE CONE	BUTTERFLY	FROG

NATURE

BINGO

MOSS	BEE	MAMMAL	WORM	DECIDUOUS TREE (LOSES LEAVES IN FALL)
ANT	BIRD	DANDELION	CONIFEROUS TREE (EVERGREEN)	SPIDER
ROCK	LADYBUG	FREE SPACE THE SKY	PINE CONE	BEETLE
THE MOON	OAK LEAF	GRASS	STAR (THE SUN COUNTS!)	FROG
MINERAL	LOG	MUSHROOM	CLOUD	BUTTERFLY

RECORD YOUR ACTIVITIES, DISCOVERIES & FINDS HERE

If you find something neat, make a sketch to the right to help you remember details so you can compare your drawing with a field guide or another reference later.

_____

_____

_____

_____

_____

_____

_____

_____

_____

_____

_____

_____

RECORD YOUR ACTIVITIES, DISCOVERIES & FINDS HERE

If you find something neat, make a sketch to the right to help you remember details so you can compare your drawing with a field guide or another reference later.

_____

_____

_____

_____

_____

_____

_____

_____

_____

_____

_____

_____

RECORD YOUR ACTIVITIES, DISCOVERIES & FINDS HERE

If you find something neat, make a sketch to the right to help you remember details so you can compare your drawing with a field guide or another reference later.

_____

_____

_____

_____

_____

_____

_____

_____

_____

_____

_____

_____

_____

RECORD YOUR ACTIVITIES, DISCOVERIES & FINDS HERE

If you find something neat, make a sketch to the right to help you remember details so you can compare your drawing with a field guide or another reference later.

_____

_____

_____

_____

_____

_____

_____

_____

_____

_____

_____

_____

_____

RECOMMENDED READING

Daniels, Jaret C. *Backyard Bugs: An Identification Guide to Common Insects, Spiders, and More.* Cambridge, Minnesota: Adventure Publications, 2017.

Daniels, Jaret C. *Wildflowers of the Southeast Field Guide.* Cambridge, Minnesota: Adventure Publications, 2012.

Lynch, Dan R. *Fossils for Kids: An Introduction to Paleontology.* Cambridge, Minnesota: Adventure Publications, 2020.

Lynch, Dan R. *Rock Collecting for Kids: An Introduction to Geology.* Cambridge, Minnesota: Adventure Publications, 2018.

Lynch, Mike. *Stars: A Month-by-Month Tour of the Constellations.* Cambridge, Minnesota: Adventure Publications, 2012.

Poppele, Jonathan. *Night Sky: A Field Guide to the Constellations.* Cambridge, Minnesota: Adventure Publications, 2009.

Sibley, David. *The Sibley Field Guide to Birds of Eastern North America.* New York: Knopf, 2016.

Tekiela, Stan. *Birds of Prey of the South Field Guide.* Cambridge, Minnesota: Adventure, 2013.

GLOSSARY

Adapted Changed in response to the environment or conditions.

Agricultural Products Farm products such as wheat, soybeans, or livestock.

Biodiverse An ecosystem that is biodiverse has a large number of plant and animal species.

Biome A community of animals and plants that live in a specific kind of climate and environment.

Chalcedony A banded form of quartz that is popular as a collectible.

Chemical Element One of the 92 naturally occurring chemicals, such as oxygen and carbon, that make up all matter on Earth.

Commodities Agricultural products (see above) that are sold worldwide.

Conifer A tree that produces seeds by cones; most conifers, but not all, are **evergreen**—that is, they stay green all winter.

Extirpated Refers to an animal or plant being eliminated from its native range.

Genus Name Because there are so many different plants and animals and other lifeforms, scientists give every organism one name, usually derived from Latin or Greek. This scientific name has two parts: a **genus name,** which is like an organism's last name and which it shares with others, and a **species name,** which is like its first name. So if you want to talk to a scientist about the American Robin, *Turdus migratorius* is the name that scientists would recognize all around the world. (And yes, that really is its scientific name.)

Introduced Brought to an area instead of occurring there naturally (example: cows in the U.S.) (Also see **Nonnative,** page 146).

Invasive Describes introduced species (see above) that outcompete native animals, harming the ecosystem.

Latitude How far north or south a person or place is from the equator; the equator is at a latitude of 0; the North Pole is 90 degrees North.

Legislature The lawmaking body (for example, the State Senate and State House of Representatives) in each Southern state; legislators are the officials who make laws pertaining to the environment.

Limestone A sedimentary rock made out of marine animals, such as coral and others; it often preserves fossils within it.

GLOSSARY

Mineral A chemical combination of two or more elements. Individual elements (such as copper and gold) are considered minerals as well.

Mohs Hardness Scale The relative scale of mineral hardness, from the softest (talc, 1) to the hardest (diamond, 10).

Mutualistic Refers to a relationship between two organisms where each one gets something of value or benefit.

Native Refers to an animal, plant, or other organism that is found naturally in an area.

Nonnative Refers to an animal, plant, or other organism that is *not* found naturally in an area. (Also see **Introduced,** page 145). **Note:** Not all nonnative plants and animals are invasive (see page 145).

Phenology The study of the seasons and other natural cycles over time.

Prescribed Fire A fire that is intentionally burned by land managers. This allows new species to thrive after the fire. Also called a **controlled fire.**

Rock A combination of two or more minerals (see above).

Saprobes Mushrooms that feed on dead or dying material (often wood or plant parts).

Second-Growth Forests Forests that grow back after old-growth forests are harvested.

Species Name See **Genus Name** (page 145).

Summer Solstice The longest day of the year, when the earth is pointed most directly at the sun; in the northern hemisphere, the summer solstice occurs in late June.

Temperate An environment where there are long periods (summer!) where the weather is warm.

Turpentine A sticky resin that comes from trees, used to make a variety of products.

Toxic Poisonous.

Waterfowl Ducks, geese, swans, and other aquatic birds.

Winter solstice The shortest day of the year, when the earth is tilted away from the sun the most; in the northern hemisphere, the summer solstice occurs in late December.

QUICK QUIZ ANSWERS

Page 5: Montgomery, Alabama; Little Rock, Arkansas; Tallahassee, Florida; Atlanta, Georgia; Frankfort, Kentucky; Baton Rouge, Louisiana; Jackson, Mississippi; Raleigh, North Carolina; Oklahoma City, Oklahoma; Columbia, South Carolina; Nashville, Tennessee; Austin, Texas; Richmond, Virginia; Charleston, West Virginia

Page 9: Fulvous Whistling-Duck

Page 11: 1. Tulip Tree 2. Sweetgum 3. Southern Red Oak

Page 13: Roseate Spoonbill

Page 15: 60

Page 31: Georgia

Page 33: Iguana

Page 55: 1. Soybeans 2. Corn 3. Sugarcane 4. Cotton

Page 91: A rock is made up of multiple minerals. This can be really confusing, because some official state rocks are actually minerals and some official minerals are actually rocks!

Page 108: 1. Eastern Calligrapher Fly 2. Yellowjacket 3. Honeybee

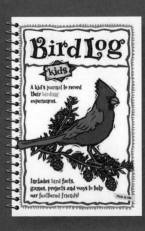
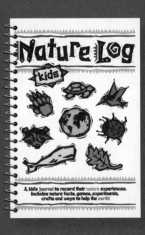

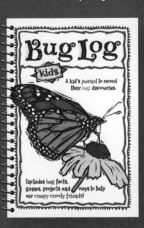

CROSSWORD ANSWERS

Page 98:

Page 115:

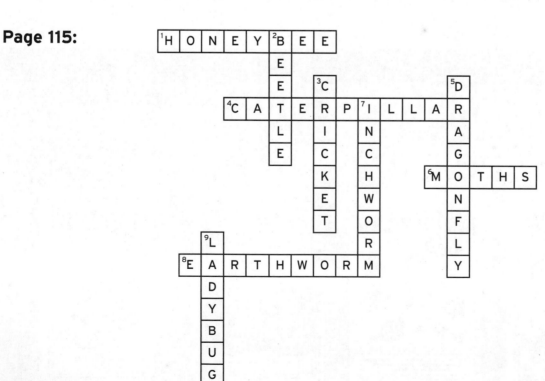

ABOUT THE AUTHOR

Erika Zambello is a writer, naturalist, and communications specialist. After earning a master's degree in environmental management from Duke University, where she specialized in ecosystem science and conservation, she traveled across the United States visiting important science and naturalist sites for the Florida Park Service, the Long Term Ecological Research Network, National Parks Traveler, NOAA, and more. Her work has appeared in *BirdWatching Daily*, *Backpacker*, *National Geographic Adventure*, *National Parks Traveler*, *Guy Harvey Magazine*, *Florida Sportsman*, and *Coastal Angler*. When she isn't working, she is exploring near her home in North Florida, looking for native bird species. She lives in Tallahassee with her husband, kid, and two cats.

ACKNOWLEDGMENTS

Thank you to my parents, who instilled in me a love of nature, and to my husband, who is always up for a new adventure.

DEDICATION

To Noah, my new favorite adventure partner.

PHOTO CREDITS

(iguanas), 33 (Quick Quiz iguana), 76 (bottom); **Jim Cumming:** 17 (Black Bear); **Jim Vallee:** 57 (Mount Cheaha); **JNix:** 55 (4); **Jo Crebbin:** 23 (Florida Panther); **John A. Anderson:** 101 (Zebra Longwing); **John L. Absher:** 22 (Scissor-Tailed Flycatcher); **Jon Bilous:** 24 (blue granite), 59 (spruce knob); **Josef Stemeseder:** 22 (Black Swallowtail); **Jovana Kuzmanovic:** 104 (centipede); **Jukka Jantunen:** 103 (Great Pondhawk); **K. Steve Cope:** 27 (Brook Trout); **Karuna Eberl:** 67; **Kim Bowman:** 94 (top), 95; **KPixMining:** 104 (Deer Tick); **Kristi Blokhin:** 76 (top); **Kristian Bell:** 25 (Gopher Tortoise); **Ksenia Lada:** 118 (Chicken of the Woods); **Kwanza Henderson:** 17 and 25 (Largemouth Bass); **Kyle Selcer:** 15; **Lara Makela:** 103 (Yellow Garden Spider); **lecsposure:** 127; **Lee Reese:** 30 (Tulip Poplar); **Leena Robinson:** 25 (Tiger Swallowtail); **LifetimeStock:** 13 (Rose-Breasted Cockatoo); **lindasky76:** 45 (left); **Lorraine Hudgins:** 88 (*Chesapecten jeffersonius*); **Love Lego:** 109 (Sweat Bees); **LutsenkoLarissa:** 30 (goldenrod); **Maarten Daams:** 53 (Bobcat); **Maclane Parker:** 18 (Largemouth Bass); **Malachi Jacobs:** 28 (rhododendron and Sugar Maple), 40 (top); **Maneerat Shotiyanpitak:** 75 (bottom right); **Manfred Ruckszio:** 102 (Colorado Potato Beetle); **Manuel Trinidad Mesa:** 50 (cotton); **Marc Goldman:** 32 (House Sparrow); **Marcel Clemens:** 23 and 85 (agatized coral); **mariakray:** 12; **Marinodenisenko:** 11 (top middle); **Mark Carey:** 87 (gold); **Mark Kostich:** 33 (American Alligator); **Markus Haberkern:** 23 (American Alligator); **Marshall Hammer:** 29 (iris); **Martin Mecnarowski:** 13 (Scarlet Ibis); **Mary A. Brenner:** 50 (Cardinal Flower); **Mary Terriberry:** 27 (American Dogwood, both), 43 (dogwoods); **McCarthy's PhotoWorks:** 96; **Melinda Fawver:** 9 (American Crow); **Michael Benard:** 102 (Reddish-Brown Stag Beetle); **Michael Fitzsimmons:** 33 (Green Anole); **Michael S. Moncrief:** 120 (Dog Vomit Slime); **Michael Siluk:** 114; **milepost430media:** 26 (dogwood); **Minakryn Ruslan:** 25 (staurolite); **mivod:** 20 (pecan); **Muhammad Naaim:** 102 (White Burrower Flathead); **Murat An:** 44; **Muskoka Stock Photos:** 102 (Goldenrod Soldier Beetle); **Nadya So:** 102 (Green June Bug); **Nagel Photography:** 25 (live oak); **Najmi Arif:** 51 (sugarcane); **Nancy J. Ondra:** 75 (bottom left); **Natalia Kuzmina:** 65, 103 (Whirligig Beetles); **natfu:** 103 (Green Lynx Spider); **nechaevkon:** 101 (mosquito); **Nick Pecker:** 29 (Tulip Poplar); **Nickolay Khoroshkov:** 40 (bottom); **Nikolay Kurzenko:** 16 (magnolia); 17 (Southern Longleaf Pine); **nito:** 50 (empty nest); **Ocollins:** 11 (top right); **Ondrej Prosicky:** 43 (Monarch Butterfly); **oticki:** 55 (1); **Pandur:** 117 (Amethyst Laccaria); **Pat Dooley:** 30 (Viceroy Butterfly); **Patty Chan:** 30 and 90 (coal); **Paul Reeves Photography:** 17 (Monarch Butterfly), 42, 103 (Candy-Striped Leafhopper), 108 (left); **Paul St. Clair:** 47 (Hooded Warbler); **Peter Turner Photography:** 11 (top left); **Photo_Traveller:** 103 (Eastern Amberwing); **PhotographyByMK:** 55 (2); **Photosbyjam:** 22 (Collared Lizard); **Piotr Velixar:** 28 and 88 (*Lithostrotionella* [Mississippian fossil coral]); **PLPelto:** 19, 83 (agate); **pote-poteco:** 17 (Oak-Leaf Hydrangea); **ppl:** 119 (coral fungi); **pr_camera:** 117 (Green-Spored Lepiota); **Frédéric Prochasson:** 39; **R. C. Bennett:** 25 (Brown Thrasher); **Radim Glajc:** 66 (coneflower); **Raul Baena:** 23 and 29 (Northern Mockingbird), 62 (Brown Pelican); **Ray Hennessy:** 19 (Brown Pelican), 50 (Black Skimmer); **Reimar:** 78; **Richard G. Smith:** 9 (Red-Tailed Hawk); **RICIfoto:** 18 (American Alligator); **River Monster Photography:** 27 (Striped Bass); **Rob Jump:** 21 (Loblolly Pine); **Robert Wilder Jr:** 14 (firefighter); **samray:** 26 (honeybee); **Sandra M. Austin:** 18 (Spice Swallowtail); **Sandrinka:** 109 (Rusty-Patched Bumblebees); **Santosh Puthran:** 26 (Carolina Lily); **Sari O'Neal:** 21 (Diana Fritillary), 47 (redbud); **Scisetti Alfio:** 24 (Yellow Jessamine); **Sean Pavone:** 58 (Brasstown Bald, GA, and Britton Hill, FL); **Sergey Tinyakov:** 71; **Shackleford Photography:** 17 and 81 (marble); **Shana D'Attilio:** 102 (Blue-Winged Olive Mayfly); **SircPhoto:** 86 (amethyst); **Somsak Nitimongkolchai:** 66 (American Beautyberry); **Stephan Hawks:** 56, 58 (Mount Magazine, AR); **Stephen B. Goodwin:** 26 (granite), 86 and 87 (granite); **Steve Bower:** 24 (Carolina Mantis), 103 (Regal Darner Dragonfly); **Steve Byland:** 18 (Northern Mockingbird), 24 (Carolina Wren), 30 (Northern Cardinal), 62 (Brown Thrasher), 66 (birdbath); **Steven Frame:** 55 (3); **stock_photo_world:** 20 (bluebonnet); **StoneMonkeyswk:** 29 (raccoon); **Sundry Photography:** 132; **Susan 78:** 47 (dogwood); **Svineyard:** 99; **Terry Kelly:** 21 (honeybee); **thecloudysunny:** 32 (Japanese Climbing Fern); **Thierry Eidenweil:** 52 (manatees); **thka:** 18, 19 and 28 (honeybee); **Thomas Barrat:** 48 (sea turtle nest); **Thoreau:** 29, 89 and 90 (Tennessee pearls); **Tiara Castillo:** 43 (blueberries); **Timothy R. Nichols:** 109 (Locust Borer Beetle); **tome213:** 17 (tarpon); **Tony Campbell:** 18 and 24 (White-Tailed Deer), 32 (feral hog); **U. Eisenloh:** 29 and 89 (limestone); **Vahan Abrahamyan:** 18 (Southern Magnolia); **Viktoryia Vinnikava:** 26 (Gray Squirrel); **Vitalina Rybakova:** 49 (blackberries); **Voinakh:** 46 (Wax Myrtle flowers); **vvoe:** 85 (moonstone); **Wildnerdpix:** 14 (top); **William Cushman:** 20 (Monarch Butterfly), 22 and 84 (Barite Rose); **Wirestock Creators:** 59 (Sassafras Mountain, SC); **Yanosh Nemesh:** 11 (bottom left); **Yinan Chen:** 53 (Purple Martins)

SAFETY NOTE

Nature is wonderful and amazing, and it's certainly nothing to be afraid of, especially if you take common-sense precautions.

This is a guide intended for backyards and green spaces in the South; such places should be pretty safe, by definition, but have an adult accompany you when outside and to supervise the activities in this book. And when you're outside, don't reach where you can't see, and be aware of potentially dangerous animals like bees, wasps, venomous spiders or snakes, and bothersome plants such as poison ivy or poison sumac/oak. While you can avoid them by paying careful attention, be especially aware if they are found in your area, or if you're allergic (to bees, for instance).

The best way to stay safe is to keep your distance from wild animals, avoid handling wildlife, and take photos or make sketches instead. Also, wear gloves, appropriate clothing for the weather, long pants in areas where ticks are present, and sunscreen (as needed). Pay attention to the weather and any potentially unsafe surroundings. You are responsible for your safety.

An important note: This book is **not** intended to help you identify which wild plants, berries, fruits, or mushrooms are safe to eat. Please leave the berries, fruits, and mushrooms you find for the birds, critters, and the bugs; instead, get your snacks from the fridge!

Edited by Brett Ortler

Cover and book design by Fallon Venable

10 9 8 7 6 5 4 3 2

Backyard Science & Discovery Workbook: South
Fun Activities and Experiments That Get Kids Outdoors
Copyright © 2021 by Erika Zambello
Published by Adventure Publications
An imprint of AdventureKEEN
310 Garfield Street South
Cambridge, Minnesota 55008
(800) 678-7006
www.adventurepublications.net
All rights reserved
Printed in China
ISBN: 978-1-64755-173-5